I end up sitting at the top of the stairs with my book open in my lap and a smile on my face.

You never really know someone until you have them inside of you. This is the last fucking thought that occurs to me before Paul "The Raging Tempest" Wolfe thrusts his cock inside of my desperately aching pussy.

I put my finger on the passage and look up at the ceiling, trying to imagine what Austin's name would be if he were some sort of professional fighter or wrestler or whatnot. I decide Austin "The Panty Melting" Sparks would be a good choice and bury my nose back in my book.

BOOKS BY
C.M. STUNICH

The Seven Wicked Series

First
Second
Third
Fourth
Fifth
Sixth
Seventh

Houses Novels

The House of Gray and Graves
The House of Hands and Hearts and Hair
The House of Sticks and Bones

The Huntswomen Trilogy

The Feed
The Hunt
The Throne

Indigo Lewis Novels

Indigo & Iris
Indigo & The Colonel
Indigo & Lynx

Never Say Never Trilogy & Never Too Late Series

Tasting Never
Finding Never
Keeping Never
Never Can Tell

Triple M Series

Losing Me, Finding You
Loving Me, Trusting You
Needing Me, Wanting You
Craving Me, Desiring You

A Duet

Paint Me Beautiful
Color Me Pretty

Craving Me, Desiring You

C.M. STUNICH

SARIAN ROYAL

to first love. to last love. and everything in between. to hearts that sing and flicker, whose words sound like wind chimes in the night. to you. thank you for reading this happily ever after.

CHAPTER 1

Austin

Beck is guffawing at me from across the damn room, and I don't know why. I scowl at him as I heft my sledgehammer up and take careful aim at a nearby wall.

"Your momma drop you on your damn head or somethin'?" he asks me through his raucous chuckling. "'Cause sometimes I think you're the stupidest motherfucker I ever laid my dang eyes on." I swing the tool at the drywall and grin big as it echoes with a satisfying crack. Pieces of old wallpaper tumble to the floor in a heap of dust. I think there are poodles or some shit on there, but I ain't looking too hard. This whole damn wall is coming down *today*. Nine weeks we been working on this fucking house, and it isn't even close to bein' done. This here, this just ain't a clubhouse, a place to hold meetings and fly our flag. This is a home for the unwanted, the men and women who don't quite fit here or there. This is a place where Amy's going to be resting her beautiful head, and I want it to be perfect. Even if I'm still unsure about it. I don't like to do things in half measures.

"And why's that?" I ask, wishing I'd just picked up the damn phone. Amy's called twice today, and I haven't answered either call. I don't know why. I guess I am just a stupid asshole. Beck runs his fingers through his red hair, grinning bigger than I've ever seen before. He's always been a happy-go-lucky son of a bitch, but ever since he picked up this girl, Tease, he's gotten even worse. Now he's a smug happy-go-lucky son of a bitch, strutting around here like a rooster that's just found the chicken coop. I ain't never seen Beck so happy. Used to think the asshole was into Melissa, but well … Melissa is into the President of Seventy-seven Brothers. Big fucking time. And Beck and Tease are like *this*.

"Why are you avoiding her phone calls?" Gaine asks, baffled at my behavior. He has more patience than I'll ever have. I take another swing at the wall, and I'm not sure I have an answer for him. It's not a question if I love Amy or not – that's not even up for discussion. I couldn't even imagine walking away from her sweet smile or her quiet laughter, the way she tucks her silken hair behind her ear. But I'm adjusting. Things are all so fucked up. Even this clubhouse thing. It makes sense for us, especially after losing so many of our own people, but it's also terrifying the ever living crap outta me. I ain't gonna lie about that.

"I'm not avoiding 'em," I say as I step back and take a deep breath. This construction shit is not easy. I managed to get a loan for the clubhouse though, ain't no such luck on getting extra money to put in all the work it needs. We're going to be paying for this with blood, sweat, and tears. "I just didn't answer them."

"Like that isn't the same damn thing?" Beck asks as he takes a swig of his water, pausing to pour some of the liquid onto his forehead with a sigh. The droplets run down his face and splatter against the plywood on the floor. We haven't gotten around to replacing that yet. It's on the tail end of a very long list, one that we're chipping away at nice and slow. "You ain't about to tuck tail and run, are you Sparks?" Beck asks me as he sets his water down, and swipes his hands down his face. He's smiling, but the look in his eyes says he isn't joking around. I scowl at him, and don't bother to answer the question. He knows me better than that.

I take another swing and the rest of the wall comes crashing down, wood beams dangling from the ceiling like spiders. I rub my arm across my face and set down the sledgehammer, moving to the window to gaze out at the empty street. This neighborhood is nothing but a rundown shit hole, full of squatters and drug addicts. There aren't any neighbors to complain about the roar of motorcycles or the raucous shouting, the comings and goings of a few dozen folk. We're turning this piss soaked house from a place to shoot up into a fucking home. Transformations. Life is all about frigging transformations. And nobody tells you how Goddamn difficult they are.

"Austin," Gaine says, this note of authority ringing clear in his voice. Ever since we sat down as a group and made him the fucking Treasurer, he's been all up in arms about this or that, shit that doesn't even have anything to do with money. I throw up my hands and pull my cellphone from my pocket.

"I'm makin' the damn call," I tell them as I push through the screen door in the back and walk through the weeds and half-brown grass. There are broken pots everywhere, along with colorful plants that look like somebody really cared about this place at one point. I glance over my shoulder, letting my eyes trail up to the third floor and the old ass windows. "Fuck me runnin'," I whisper under my breath, running my hands up the sides of my face. I haven't shaved in a couple of days, but Amy seems to like it. Or at least I think she does. Sometimes, I'm too afraid to ask what those cute little half-smiles mean. I dial my baby up and wait.

"Austin," she breathes, answering the call on a sharp intake of air. I feel the word straight down to my toes – most especially in the area of my crotch. "How's your day been?" Amy doesn't wait for me to answer, just continues on like she can't bear to hold in the news. "I've heard the most marvelous thing today." Amy pauses abruptly, and I can just imagine her squeezing her eyes shut tight. "But I can't tell you. It's not my news to share."

I laugh. How could I not? Amy makes me want to smile, to see life in a different light. You ever hear the phrase *rose colored glasses*? That's how she tints the world for me.

"Then why you callin' me, sugar?" I ask, examining the fresh white paint on the outside of the house. This here's a historical wonder, apparently, and we had to take the high route. No vinyl siding for this baby. We had to sand down and repair the original wood siding. During the act, all I could think was that it was a pain in the ass. Right now, I'm feelin' pretty prideful. "Today's your day off. You shouldn't even be thinking of me." I can hear Amy smiling when she next speaks.

"A day off without you isn't much of a day off at all."

She pauses. "I'm having a good time with the girls, but I miss you. Is that stupid?" I turn away from the house and poke at a bit of broken statue with my boot. Her words do two opposite things to me. On the one hand, I want to jump for joy and clack my damn heels. On the other, my heart starts to beat and this sickening creep of doubt reaches inside my chest. It's started happening to me lately, on and off. Ever since Kent died. *Since you killed him, Sparks.* When I walked into that room and saw Amy bleeding, I just went bat shit. I won't apologize for that. Still, the unrest that's been plaguing us ever since is getting old.

"Not stupid at all, sugar. The job site's just not the same without you." I smirk and bring up a lurid little image of me and Amy pressed into the tiny downstairs bathroom. *Hot damn.* I keep thinking that at some point, the sex won't be as good or I won't find Amy as hot, but it never happens. At least not on my end. There's always the chance that little Miss Amy could get sick and tired of my ugly, ol' ass. "But hey, absence makes the heart grow fonder." I grin and switch the phone to my other ear. "And the cock stiffer. I hope you're ready for me when I get back." Amy chuckles as I glance over my shoulder. My friends have a nasty habit of sneaking up on me when I'm not looking. Nosier than a couple of old cat ladies. Christ in

Heaven.

"Austin," Amy says again, keeping her voice calm and focused. "I called you earlier today because I wanted to ask you something ... " She trails off, and I just know she's biting at that glossy lower lip of hers. I'm starting to learn all of Amy's habits – the way she talks with her hands, the way her hair falls when she tucks it behind her ear – so even though she's not standing here, I can *see* her. Sounds lame as hell, right? I walk in a small circle, tripping over a cluster of rocks that probably served as a fire pit at some point. I ain't paying attention, and that's not good for anybody or anything. "But you didn't answer, so I ... I made an executive decision." Amy clears her throat, and I feel guilty for avoiding her call.

"Dish the dirt, sugar," I tell her as Beck appears in the open doorway, folding his arms over his broad chest. He's grinning, as usual. I flip him off and push some sandy hair away from my face. Might be time to cut that fuckin' shit.

"I bought a bike, Austin," Amy breathes, and chills break out down my spine. "It wasn't planned," she rushes, trying to explain as my heart picks up speed and begins to thump inside my chest. "We went looking and it ... it just chose me." She sucks in a deep breath. "Please don't be angry." Despite everything, I find myself smiling. *My little Southern belle has turned into a real biker chick, huh?*

"Hey, if the pull of the road's not the most powerful thing there is, then I'm a lyin' man, and my momma raised me better than that. You take her for a ride yet?" I ask, hoping the answer's no. I don't know why, but I feel like I've gotta be there for the moment Amy Cross takes off on her first ride, bursts through the sunset and disappears down an open stretch of road. That there's a monumental moment.

"Excuse me, Mr. Sparks, but I seem to recall you saying the only thing you'd like to ride cross-country would be a *she*. Well, the only thing *I* would like to ride cross-country is a *he*. Henceforth, you shall refer to my ride as Sir."

CHAPTER 2

I've always enjoyed the twilight. The rippling purple colors of the night sky clash with the bright orange and pink of the setting sun, giving rise to the belief that out there, somewhere, there's a whole other world ready to be explored. I simply don't see how someone could stand here and look at this ethereal beauty without being completely and utterly convinced of an afterlife. I don't pretend to know what it entails, only that one exists. Beauty like this simply never dies.

I sweep some hair away from my face and keep my book clutched tight in my hand. I ponder the last words in my chapter as I examine the clouds floating weightless above me.

"Sali, I'll never be good enough for you," Glance

C.M. Stunich

*Serone says as he gazes out the floor to ceiling windows
in my new apartment. The apartment that he bought for
me, where he laid me out and made the sweetest love to
me. Glance. The world's biggest asshole, and the only
man capable of melting my heart.*

My absolute favorite book in the world has a new
sequel, I've got a new bike, and the only man capable of
melting *my* heart is riding straight towards me on the
back of his motorcycle. I adjust myself on the seat,
enjoying the comforting squeak of leather on leather.
Yes, that's right. You heard me: Amy Allison Cross is
wearing leather pants. And they look quite good on
me, thank you very much.

A soft breeze kisses my face, its gentleness at odds
with the rough growl of the boys' bikes as they move
down the road towards us, sliding into the gravel
parking lot like a pack of wolves. *And my lover is the
alpha*, I think with a flurry of goose bumps across my
bare arms. The night is warm, the remnants of the
summer sun kissing my skin like butterflies. I close my
book and set it aside, swinging myself off my bike as
Austin skids to a stop and grins big at me.

"Well, hello, Sir," Austin drawls, moving towards me
and breezing past like he hardly notices me. My mouth
twitches to match his smile as I spin after him and
watch while Austin, Beck, and Gaine circle my new ride

like sharks. "Harley-Davidson. Can never go wrong with that." Austin bends low and runs his hands over the shiny crimson paint. "A Sportster, huh?"

"A Sportster Superlow," Kimmi interjects, approaching with Mireya and Christy at her heels. Kimmi is beaming from ear to ear, her gold earrings catching the last rays of the setting sun as she pauses near the handlebars and touches her fingers to the chrome on the back of the mirror. "A perfect sized ride for Miss Amy, don't you think?"

"And it was a steal, too," Mireya drones, waving her hand dismissively. I notice she doesn't leave her new bike's side, pressing the length of her thigh against the metal for comfort. "Blah, blah, blah. Enough with the babble. Are we going to take it for a test drive or not?" She sounds angry, but I can tell it's all false bravado. Since she eloped with Gaine, Mireya's actually been fairly nice to me. I think we might manage to be friends one day.

I twist my hands nervously and run my tongue over my lips. I know Austin and Kimmi's last hit made the club a lot of money, but then again, we just bought a house. I hope he isn't going to be angry with me. I take a step closer and watch his brown eyes raise to mine.

He's still smiling.

"What do you think?" I ask, waiting with nervous

anticipation for Austin to close the gap between us and take me in his arms. I crave his touch even more now than I did before. The initial attraction still burns between us, but I can feel a deeper ache down below, something that tells me this will only get better with age. How can I possibly know if he feels the same? We've never actually said those words to one another. *I love you.*

I spare a glance for Beck and Tease, making out like teenagers a few steps away from where I stand. They said it, and they've only just met, but that's okay. If I've learned anything from reading romance novels, it's that love never happens in quite the same way. Sometimes, it's a slow, burning ache, and others, it's a rapid-fire feast for the heart. I don't judge any form of love to be higher or lower than any other.

I swing my gaze back to Austin just in time to see him moving towards me.

"If Mireya says it's a good ride, then it's a good ride," Gaine says with a smile, giving his new wife a come-hither look that makes her bristle and frown. But only on the outside. In her dark eyes, I can see it. Love. Love, love, love. It's blooming and blossoming all around us.

I look up at Austin, shivering as he runs his fingers down my bare arms.

"I think I remember tellin' you somethin' about pants," he whispers against my ear. My eyes flutter closed and I swoon into his arms. Just like a heroine in one of my books. His body is rock hard and warm, and he smells like sweat and dirt. It's as decidedly delicious as it sounds. "As in, you should never wear 'em. I don't like obstacles in my way, sugar."

"But we're going for a ride," I whisper as I lean back, pressing the full length of my body against his. I can feel Austin's erection grinding into my belly as I recline in his arms, letting my hair spill down my back as he presses his hot lips to my throat. Vaguely, I realize that some of the other Triple M'ers are catcalling at us from the edges of the parking lot, but I don't care. When I'm standing here, like this, nothing else matters. "You ... you promised," I moan, almost wishing that he hadn't.

"Did I?" Austin asks, pulling back and steadying me on my feet. I touch my fingers to his dirty T-shirt, brushing some of the white dust from his shoulders. I keep my gaze on his pecs instead of on his face. I'm afraid that if I look up into those eyes, I'll start falling and I won't be able to catch myself.

"Ride first, fuck later," Kimmi groans from behind Austin. "We don't all have partners for the evening." I hear a burst of sharp, nervous laughter from Christy's throat, and I imagine that she's staring at the wild

13

redhead in two parts fear and one part awe. I don't want to push my friend towards Kimmi simply because she's Austin's best friend, or even because they're the only two lesbians in the group, but they would make a cute couple ...

"Yeah, yeah, we hear ya," Beck chortles, clapping his hand on his friend's back. Kimmi narrows her green eyes at him and adjusts her jacket on her shoulders as Austin pulls away from me with a sigh. I try not to pout, but it's oh so difficult to let go of a man who simply looks like Adonis incarnate – only a little blonder, and with slightly less curly hair. "Besides, nothing gets the blood pumpin' like a good, long ride."

"And how do I know you're not actually referring to the motorcycles?" Kimmi asks with a pursed mouth. She licks her tongue over her red lips and gestures at the back of her bike while Beck laughs and swings Tease up into his arms like she weighs nothing. I think of the exciting news she shared with me today, and I can hardly keep the words contained. *Tease is pregnant!* I want to shout, because who doesn't love a baby? But she hasn't told Beck yet, so I keep my lips sealed. She's promised to tell him tonight. I smile at them and for the first time in my life, I don't have to wonder what it's like to fall in love so fast, to race through the world at a dizzying speed and land in the universe's most deliciously decadent trap. "Christy, you're welcome to ride with me if you want to come?" Kimmi asks, acting suspiciously nonchalant.

My friend shakes her head and smiles, her blonde hair falling to obscure her face.

"No, that's alright. I'm going to hang out by the pool." Christy glances up sharply and catches my gaze. I imagine that I might be imitating my mother's best *oh, no you don't* look, but I can't help it. I find that the more time I spend away from her, the more I recognize her better qualities and begin to imitate them. I imitate nothing of my father's.

"We can swim when we get back," I say, trying to make a point. Christy is not doing as well here as I am. She's having a hell of a lot harder time adjusting. I realize I probably don't make it easy spending so much time with Austin, and vow to myself that I'll take a day sometime this week for just me and her. All day today, we hung out in a group with Kimmi, Mireya, and Tease, exploring this town that's soon to be our home. Some alone time is in order. "It's like flying, Christy," I whisper, my words getting caught on the wind and fluttering like the strands of loose hair around my face.

"I know," she says, but she doesn't elaborate. I can't claim she hasn't given it a try. She's been traveling around with the rest of us for the past few months.

"But I … it scares me a little bit."

"Scares you?" Kimmi shouts, touching her hands to either side of her face. "Girl, you picked the wrong lifestyle if a motorcycle scares you." I watch as Kimmi reaches out her hand, wrapping her fingers around Christy's thin wrist and tugging her forward. "Come on. There's nothing to fear but fear itself."

CHAPTER 3

The wind bites at my face because although I'm wearing the helmet, I refuse to put down the visor. The sunglasses I borrowed from Kimmi keep the worst of it out of my eyes, but I would not be surprised if I ended up accidentally swallowing a bug or two. It doesn't matter though, nothing does, not when the world looks like this.

I speed towards the brightness on the horizon, knowing that Austin is probably grinding his teeth watching me go this fast but unable to stop myself. *Pure bliss*, I think as I come up on a curve and slow down, leaning into it and trying my best to remember all the things Austin taught me. He's let me drive his bike a few times, but only on dirty old back roads and only, only, only if he's riding behind me. Today, I'm on my own and the absence of his arms around my waist is both a sin and a pleasure. It might not be a big thing to some people, but the fact that I'm here, that I'm controlling this massive hunk of metal between my thighs, that's a big accomplishment for me. It's one of the few things I've ever done on my own. *Besides sleeping with Austin*, I think with a smile. *Or running away to join a motorcycle club.*

I relish the feel of the leather jacket on my shoulders, and I don't even care that it says *Prospect* on the back of it. I belong. Not just in body, but in soul. Recent tragedies aside, Austin Sparks and Triple M have been like a dream for me.

I hit a flat stretch of road and try not to laugh with maniacal pleasure. Certainly that would be very unladylike.

"This is fucking incredible!" I shout into the mic on my helmet, and the words feel so good spilling from my lips that I say it again. "In-fucking-credible." Laughter tickles my ears as Beck bursts onto the line with a snort.

"Second best thing next to an orgasm, I always say."

"Shut your damn mouth, Beck, and let her concentrate," Austin says, and my heart swells at the protective note in his voice. But even though I want him to protect me, I also want to be able to stand on my own two feet. I run my tongue over my lips and pick up speed, feeling like a goddess of the open road. For just the briefest of nanoseconds, I close my eyes and imagine that there are wings on my back, made of dark leather that creaks as they unfold behind me in a wave of blackness.

I flick my eyes back open and shoot past a farmhouse and a field of white flowers that are just barely visible in the waning light of day. I don't really know where I'm going or what I'm doing until I come to the exit that would take me home. I slow to a stop and pause on the side of the road, dragging my friends along with me as I remove my helmet and my sunglasses.

"Everything okay there, darlin'?" Austin asks from beside me. I touch my fingers to my belly, listening to the uneasy roil of my stomach. I'm miles and miles away from home – I'm not positive on the exact distance – but I know that if I were to roll this bike up the ramp, I would be there before night struck me a second time. I look away from the sign for the exit and try to smile at Austin. I find it odd that I'm behaving this way considering I passed through Wilkes to get Christy. I barely left the hotel, and I most certainly did not speak with anyone else I knew, but I was there and it didn't feel like this. Maybe it's because we're planning on staying in one place for awhile? While I was traveling, I could almost pretend there was no such thing as *home*, like it never even existed to begin with. Sometimes, standing still is harder than moving forward. I'm not sure, but I don't like this uncomfortable queasiness that's settled over me.

"Everything's fine," I tell Austin, putting my sunglasses and my helmet back on. *It is*, I tell myself firmly. *Everything is fine, but soon I might have to deal with demons from my past. Namely, my parents.* That makes me smile a bit wider. My father would not do well to learn I'd compared him to a demonic entity of any sort.

"Good," he says, leaning over and pressing a kiss to my check. His stubble scrapes across my skin and makes my fingers clench tight against the leather of my pants. "Because I got big plans for you when we get back to the hotel. Wouldn't want any emotional crises to interfere with all the nasty things I plan to do to you." He grins as he pulls away, pausing a moment to pull his phone from his pocket. I hear Gaine groan from behind us as the Nickelback ringtone plays sharply in the empty air. "Sparks," he says, holding it up to his ear. It only takes a split second for his grin to morph into an angry frown. "We'll be right there," he snaps, hanging up and pulling down his visor before I get a chance to ask what's going on. When I hear his next words, any thoughts of my parents or my hometown vanish into the background of my mind. "Time to head to the clubhouse. We got trouble."

CHAPTER 4
Austin

I ain't ever been all that good at math, but four plus four equals eight. I'm pretty sure of that. And I'm also pretty fucking sure that eight is less than sixty. If my arithmetic hasn't failed me, then I know one thing for sure: Broken Dallas has got us grossly outnumbered. The four guys we got in the house, plus Beck, Mireya, Gaine and me. Not exactly a fair match.

"Fuck me up the Goddamn creek behind my grandmomma's house. Shoot," Beck snarls, running his hand through his red hair and tossing his helmet angrily to the rough patch of grass that serves as a backyard to the abandoned house we're crouching next to. "How much longer till the rest of our assholes show up?" I check my phone with a frown.

"Fifteen minutes," I say, but it don't really matter anyway. Even if we had all our able-bodied members here, we'd still be outnumbered. "The last thing we need is another shoot-out." I can't stop thinking about the ten members we lost in the fight with Seventy-seven Brothers. It's on my mind half the damn time, and I don't know how to get over that. *Margot, you fucking bitch. I hope you got everything you deserved.* It damn near killed me to let her walk away, but it had to be done. *I've gotta start thinking like a leader and not just a man. Men and leaders make different choices, or at least they* should. "I don't want this to turn into an all out bloodbath," I whisper roughly, rising to my feet and ducking out of view of the street.

Broken Dallas is back and they've brought reinforcements. *Fuck.* This was bound to happen at some point. I was just hoping it would be after we were settled in and had some more members to swell our ranks. Guess I should've picked a house they'd never been to before. 'Spose they would've found us eventually though. The Code of the Road demands retribution for wrongs committed.

"Christ." I run my hand through my hair and look over at Gaine and Mireya whispering near the back porch of this other house. Not everyone knows what I've done, but I bought this one, too. Or rather, Kimmi bought this one. Didn't think we were going to fit forty assholes in one house, right? Not even if it's got fifteen fuckin' bedrooms. I've been president for less than two months and already, I got delusions o' grandeur. I lean against the wall and close my eyes tight. That feeling is back again – insecurity. That's what it is, and I don't like it. For years, we did things one way in Triple M. We traveled, we robbed banks, and I fucked whomever I wanted whenever I wanted. This new life is a 180, and the turn is makin' me dizzy.

"You want me to sneak up on 'em and grab another hostage?" Beck asks, but he knows as well as I do that that won't work. Not permanently. We need another plan and, as President, it's my job to come up with something. I open my eyes and glance over at my friend, dressed in a tight red T-shirt. It looks like it's painted on his damn chest. Never saw him wear anything like that before. I imagine that it's Tease's doing.

Something clicks into place.

Tease. Seventy-seven Brothers. Melissa.

It's a long shot, but that's better than no shot at all.

I push away from the wall and slide my cell out of my pocket. Hopefully the former Mrs. Diamond is in a giving mood. I dial her up and pray she's still got her Triple M phone on her.

"I haven't even been gone three months and already, you miss me so much it hurts," Melissa purrs into the phone. My fist clenches at my side, but I force myself to relax. This is a *good* sign. If she's acting like her old, flirty self then she might – *might* – be inclined to try to help us.

"Nice to hear your voice, sugar," I say, watching as Beck's brows raise in a question. "How are you enjoying your time as Tax's new ol' lady?" I watch a grin break out across my friend's face. Pretty dang sure he and Melissa have been keeping in touch this whole time.

"I was born to be a President's wife, you know that," she says, pausing to take a sip of something. "So what is it that you want? Obviously you aren't calling just to lip flap at me."

"Well," I say, peering around the corner at the circle of bikes in the street. Nobody's moving, just standing around drinking beer and smoking cigarettes. Somebody's even set up a stereo, filling the abandoned neighborhood up with old rock music. Motherfuckers. I ain't about to sit here and watch a rival gang have a tailgating party in my front yard. I look up at the house, but it's dark and there's no sign of the four Triple M'ers that are inside. "How well you and this Tax guy hittin' it off?"

"Did you not hear me, Austin Sparks? I said *wife*. I meant *wife*. This is not a figurative term." Just over two months in and she's already married the guy? I always knew that woman was trouble. I resist the urge to ask if she's over Kent yet. "Why? What do you want from Tax?"

"What's his current opinion on Broken Dallas?" I ask, edging my way into the real question. *Are you willing to help us out here*? I don't like to prey on anybody's weakness, but we do have Tax's little sister here and from his previous actions, I know that he cares a whole hell of a lot about her. I'm not about to threaten the girl or nothing, but maybe since she's a member of our club now, Tax'll be willing to give us a hand here.

"Why?" Melissa asks, her voice all hard edges and broken glass. I lick my chapped lips and think of Amy. I'm gonna need all the strength I got to stretch my pride and ask for help from a woman I spent years despising. I look at Beck's face and focus on his green eyes. Stupid asshole. He always liked Melissa, and the man's a good judge of character, so I think maybe he sees something in her that I don't. I try to take comfort in that.

"They got every able-bodied man in their group surrounding my damn clubhouse." I wait for laughter, or a rude remark or somethin' that the old Melissa would do. Instead, all I get is silence.

"Let me talk to him, and I'll call you back." The phone goes dead and I drop it to my side with a sigh.

"Well?" Beck asks, tucking his hands in his pockets and brimming with unrestrained energy. If I let him loose, he would *destroy*. I bet he'd take down a dozen dudes before they managed to fill his ass full of holes. "What did she say?"

"You're asking Melissa for help?" Mireya asks with a sneer. Her dark eyes gleam with irritation. "Like we can't fight our own battles? Seventy-seven Brothers *killed* ten of our people. Shot 'em dead. And yeah." She raises her hands. "Yeah, they might have been set off by Margot, and maybe she was working for Broken Dallas or Bested by Crows or who the fuck ever, but that doesn't change the fact that their guns, their knives, their hands murdered our family members."

"Doesn't change the fact that we did the same right back at them, sugar lips," Beck says, getting out a cigarette and moving over to the front porch so Broken Dallas won't see the smoke. "That I stabbed their Sergeant at arms to death." Beck shrugs and leans over, putting his elbow on his knee. There's a half-smile on his face that promises violence. I don't envy those motherfuckers over there.

"We don't really have a whole lot of other choices,"

Gaine says with a frown. The T-shirt he's got on today says *Born Screwed and Raised Wrong.* Interesting choice. Mireya snarls somethin' nasty under her breath, and I'm thankful I don't speak Spanish. I don't want to know what she's sayin'.

"You want to take them all out or something?" she asks, and I shrug. I haven't thought that far. It all depends on what Seventy-seven Brothers is willing to offer us. I still have that sick feeling in my stomach and a rough notion that this crap isn't going to be over until it's over. Broken Dallas might have to go. Same thing with Bested by Crows. I can't live my whole life worried they're going to ride over the horizon and fuck with us. I guess the best case scenario would be to add to our ranks, become more of a thorn in their sides than they are in ours. "*Hijo de puta,*" Mireya growls at me as she stalks away and pauses with her gaze facing towards the highway.

"Call the crew and tell 'em to hold back," I tell Gaine, stalking across the massive backyard and moving along the back fence, testing the shoddy wooden boards with my foot. Sure enough, most of them are loose and easy to fuck around with. I pry some off and slip through, into the dog run that lines the back lot of the other house. Once I'm inside, it's easy to find a spot to peer through and grab a glimpse of the yard and the back of the house. Both gates leading into the front yard are open, giving me a clear shot to the street. If it comes down to it, I'll have my guys sneak out the back and join me here. We can take a few potshots at these assholes.

My phone vibrates, and I answer it before it can draw any attention my way.

"Austin Sparks?" It's not Melissa.

"Good evening, Tax," I whisper, crawling back through the fence and moving towards my friends. The sun's just about disappeared, and all we've got for light is spotty street lamps dotting the sky with spots of orange. Half of them are dim, and a good quarter of them are out completely. This ain't the most ideal scenario to be in. Shadows crawl around me, giving me chills down my spine. I don't want to lose another member of this group. When I do, it feels like little pieces of my soul are being stripped away. It's a mighty uncomfortable feeling.

"I take it I can speak freely?" he asks, his voice hard. I have no idea what to expect. Maybe a good ass chewing, telling me to take my trouble elsewhere? Who the fuck knows?

"Of course," I say, getting out a cigarette of my own and staring across the street into the empty eyes of a broken house. This one's in even worse repair than the two we bought. Half the windows are blown out, and there's graffiti streaming down the siding in a colorful array of curse words and swirling symbols I won't even begin to try to decipher. Hope these thugs know that this ain't their territory anymore. This city belongs to Triple M now. *Provided you can get your shit together, Sparks. You're already asking for help, and you ain't even moved in yet.* I push aside the thought and think about the now. The later will have to wait. The world is full of people who don't belong, folks lookin' for something different. I don't imagine us having a hard time finding a few of them to don our Triple M's.

"I – *we* – haven't forgiven you for what happened, and I'm sure you haven't forgiven us either." Tax takes a deep breath. "So, no, we won't drive our crew down their and interfere on your behalf." I wait, my hand clenching the phone so hard, I'm afraid for a second there that I might break the damn thing. "But we also have a saying. *Should the Need Arise.* Well, the need has fucking arisen. That girl, Margot, she's fucking *gone.*" I feel my blood go cold.

"Gone?" I ask, praying that Amy and Kimmi are okay back at the hotel. Now that our rat's been flushed out of the group, they should be safe, but you never know. People have ways of finding shit out. For all I know, there could be another group of guys heading that way. I grit my teeth and pray for this night to end soon.

"I don't take torture or murder lightly, Mr. Sparks. I was going to give the girl a fair trial, but she disappeared just a few days after we picked her up. She didn't knock four of my men out on her own." Tax's voice drops low, into a growl. "So I don't know if she's with Broken Dallas, but I can take an educated guess based on what you told us. It's either them or Bested by Crows or both, but I don't give a shit. They contributed to the incident in Korbin, so extracting a price is less of a question and more of a requirement."

"So you are coming then?" I ask, trying to wrap my head around this shit.

"I'm asking you a favor, from one President to another, to please let them know that we're on our way and that we'd like to have a talk. That's it. Nothing more, nothing less. We'll be arriving in town in the morning, provided that's alright with you?" Tax is asking my permission, like this turf is already pissed on and marked as my own. It feels good, won't lie about that. The uneasy feeling in my stomach subsides for a moment, and I feel a grin light my face, a smile to rival even Beck's.

"It would be my pleasure."

CHAPTER 5
Austin

I've got my friends at my back, and my enemies in front. I've still got four guys in the house, and fifteen in the dog run that lines the back of the property. There are ten more Triple M'ers on the other side of the street, crouching in the shadows of abandoned yards.

"About time you showed up," one of the men says. He has a long silver beard and a rugged face that I'm starting to recognize. We've met one too many times, this guy and me. "We were starting to wonder if it might just be best to burn the house to the ground and let bygones be bygones."

I pause, making sure I'm underneath a streetlight, so the asshole can see the smile on my face.

"If we're gonna keep meetin' like this, I think it'd be

nice to get to know one another. My name is Austin Sparks, but I think you knew that." I put my hands on my hips and enjoy the way the man's eyes lock onto Beck. Oh, he remembers 'im alright. "Now, it's your turn. State your name, and explain to me why you think it's alright to camp out on our front lawn." I can barely see the man smile through his tangled beard. His dark eyes are like shadows, the dim light from above highlighting the crags of his face but doing little to illuminate it. I just stand there and take comfort in the gun at my hip and the crazy asshole at my side.

"Oh, I don't know," he says, running his rough fingers down his beard. "I think you lost your chance for pleasantries when that redheaded fuck disrespected me and my club. I think we'd better stick to strict business here."

"And what's that?" I ask, feeling the tension bubble around me, desperate to erupt. My people never got to take their anger out on anyone for the shooting, and they're itching for it. I hope nobody's finger accidentally twitches on no trigger. I keep the smile on my face.

"Same demands as before, except this time, the price has doubled. We want your bitches, we want their cuts, and we want double the amount we were asking for before. You can make your first payment when we return the girls after a fun filled weekend out." The man pauses and glances around at his men. Most of them are impassive, like they ain't got feelings or fucking balls in their ragged ass pants. No real man would ever want a lady that didn't want him back. It takes bigger balls to respect a woman and show her your pride than it does to belittle and intimidate. I've known that for a long time, but some folks are slow on the uptake. I resist the urge to growl when he continues speaking. "Or, we could fight it out, shed some blood, and see who comes out on top. I can't imagine that you've got much of a choice here. Bested by Crows has a new president, and they're ready to speak with you about Kent's death. I imagine they'll be here sometime tomorrow." Silver Beard grins at me, making my lip curl unconsciously to the side. *Fuck my stars. This is not good news.*

"You come here saying you want to uphold your brotherhood, but you don't realize that we got a sisterhood with these girls. What you're asking isn't going to happen, so you can shoot us if you want." I glance over at Beck. "Or at least, you can try, but first, I've got a message for you." I try to keep the glee out of my voice when I speak. "Seventy-seven Brothers is on their way, and they've also got some business they'd like to discuss with you." I let the implications linger in the air, and I don't miss the twitch in Mr. Silver Beard's cheek when Beck starts to laugh his ass off.

CHAPTER 6

"Are you tense?" I ask Austin, running my fingers over his bare shoulders. "You feel tense." I don't miss the way his hands clench on the bedspread as I press my breasts against his back and lean over to kiss his ear. It's embarrassing to admit, but flirting and kissing and lovemaking, those are skills like any other and I think I've gotten quite good at them. After all, I have had quite a bit of practice. "You won't tell me what's going on, so I have no way to judge your mood."

"I don't want you to worry your pretty little head about it," Austin says mildly. I can tell though, his mind is far, far away. I resolve to change that. I slide my hands forward and continue down his chest, feeling the hard points of his nipples as my palms glide over them. He shudders in my arms as I smile down at the rising bulge in his pants. And I only blush a slight bit while doing it.

"You said we could be partners. You told me I could be more than an ... than an *old lady* to you," I say, and the words sound strange coming out of my mouth. I might be catching on quick, but I'm still a newcomer to this world. The terminology doesn't flow as freely from my mouth as it does from Kimmi's or Mireya's. I imagine that one day it will though. Austin sighs and leans into me, looking up through a fall of sandy blonde hair that I find just as attractive as the day I met him. I run my fingers of my right hand through it.

"Do you ever worry that you're not good enough?" Austin asks, letting his eyes fall closed for a moment. I stare at his face, at the tiny scar on his lip, the golden stubble along his jaw, and I can't figure out what he means.

"How so?" I ask as he sighs and reaches up, clasping his large hands around my small ones.

"Just ... not good enough," he breathes, opening his brown eyes and putting on a smile that I know must be fake. You don't ask a question that profound and suddenly feel happy about it.

"Austin," I begin, but he's already chuckling and

releasing me, turning around and pulling me onto his lap as we perch on the end of the floral drenched bed. The look in his face has changed from contemplative to hungry. I swallow hard and try not to think too hard about the ending of my book. Sali and Glance's final chapter had me sweating so profusely that Kimmi stopped her pacing and worrying to stare at me with wide eyes. She'd thought I had a fever or something. When I think about what they did in those deliciously sultry pages, I *feel* feverish. "Austin," I say again, but my voice comes out shallow and breathy, making my stomach tighten almost imperceptibly.

"It's gettin' late," he purrs, nuzzling against my throat and scraping the smooth skin with his stubbled jaw. A sizzling kiss follows, burning my skin and drawing a gasp from my throat. "I reckon we better be climbing into bed. We've got an early start in the morning." Austin brings his face back to mine and presses his mouth against my lips. I moan against his kiss, arching my back when his hand finds my breast. *From virgin to sex Goddess – I certainly have come a long way.*

I kiss him back, trying to put into my tongue the feelings that won't come out of my mouth any other way. *I love you*, I think at him, wishing he'd say it first. I so desperately want him to. We're bound together now, he and I. I feel like our souls are tangled, but I still won't say it first. If anything, my favorite book character, Sali Bend, has made me quite wary of blurting out those three words. *I've only said the L-word three times in my life and every time it ended the same way: with a rugged kiss and an excuse about the time. I never did see any of those men again.* Not that I think Austin would run off and leave me, but still. Maybe I'm just a coward? Maybe that's it?

"Maybe we *should* get into bed," I admit to him, pulling back from his mouth just long enough to say the words. Austin grins and plants another big one right on my mouth before depositing me onto the bed and rising to his feet. I keep my gaze locked into the skull tattoo on the center of his chest as he backs up and, with a dirty grin and a chuckle, flicks the switch on the lights.

The room falls into perfect darkness, broken only by the single shaft of moonlight that penetrates the room from the crack in the curtains. I feel suddenly tense, like my skin is stretched tight across my bones. My body thrums with excitement and nervousness as my eyes adjust, and I try to spy Austin coming across the room towards me. I catch a glimpse of him as he steps into the moonlight, unbuttoning his pants and sliding them over his hips. The three M tattoos on his body tease me mercilessly as I close my eyes and lean my head back. Father always used to preach that sex outside of marriage was a sin, but if that's true, then this is the dirtiest, most delicious sin there is. *I would risk the fires of hell for you, Austin Sparks,* I think as the bed creaks and he appears above me, all hard muscles and sharp lines.

"You are so fucking hot, Miss Cross," he says, and his voice, while strong and dripping with need, has a hint of uncertainty in it that I don't like. I think it must be because of whatever happened today, and I never dream that it has anything to do with me.

I clear my throat.

"Right back at you, Mr. Sparks," I say as he reaches his right hand down and slides it up my thigh. Thrills of intense pleasure rocket through my nerve endings, frying my poor brain before we've even really gotten started. His warm hand is a nice contrast against the coolness of the air conditioned room.

"Talk nasty to me, sweetness," he whispers as his hand travels up and finds my nonexistent underwear. I've taken to forgoing panties as of late. They seem to do more harm than good.

"I'm not very good at it," I say, feeling my cheeks heat. Mostly, I tell him this because I'm embarrassed and not because I really think I'm lacking any skill. My books have taught me well. I swallow and lift my arms up, allowing Austin to pull my nightgown over my head. "But I'll try if you'd like."

"Oh, I'd like it alright," he growls, bending low, tasting my ear with his tongue. He keeps this frustrating distance between our bodies, his cock hovering close to my opening but not touching me. His chest is several inches above mine, and it's infuriating. I want to feel his body pressing me into the bed, covering me with his hard heat and his tight muscles. I wind my fingers together behind his neck and try to pull him to me. "Not yet, sugar," he whispers. "Not until you beg for it." I make a false pout with my lips, but I don't know if he can see me with his face already halfway to my bare breasts. Hit breath tickles my nipples and before I can utter a single word, he's massaging me with his tongue, tasting me and pulling a harsh gasp from my throat.

"Be gentle with them," I whisper. "They're sore." All that gets me is a growl and the scrape of teeth. My eyes flutter and I feel like I'm about to pass out. My breasts *are* sore, but it feels so good I can't bear to ask him to stop. Austin settles himself down, lighting my body on fire where our skin touches, but he doesn't enter me. Instead he keeps kissing his way down, pausing at my belly button in an agonizing display of self-control.

"That ain't much of a plea," he says, holding my hips with his hands and pressing small kisses to the lines of my pelvic bone. "Are you sure you really want it?"

"I do," I whisper, pausing to pull Sali's words again. One day, I'm sure I'll find some of my own, but for right now, this will have to do. "Fuck me until I can barely stand," I say, and then flush from head to toe. Good thing the lights are off. I may be able to retain some of my dignity this way. Austin moves between my thighs with another growl of pleasure, pressing his mouth to my opening and teasing me with his tongue.

Lights sparkle beneath my eyelids, and I swear, I'm halfway to orgasming already.

"Fuck me until I can barely breathe. Until I suffocate and drown in the ... " Sali tells Glance she wants to drown in the *throes of his undying love*, but I'm not I'm prepared to toss that statement out, so I switch things up a bit. "Heat of your passion."

Austin laughs, a full on belly laugh and pulls away for a moment. I grab at his hair and tangle my fist in the sandy blonde strands.

"If you stop, Mr. Sparks, I swear on this depths of this earth that I'm going to be *fucking pissed* at you." If I'd known curse words felt like silk fluttering across your lips every time you said them, I would've started mouthing off in the third grade.

"Oh, you want me to keep going?" he asks, and although I can't quite see the grin on his face in the darkness, I can hear it. "I thought you were quoting a damn Shakespeare poem or somethin'."

"I could if you wanted," I tell him haughtily, pulling his head up and feeling my heart speed up as our chests align. *I want to feel his, too, to know that it's beating for me the way mine beats for him. Fuck. I just want him to say* I love you, Amy. "*Shall I compare thee to a summer's day/thou art more lovely and more temperate.*"

"You smart-mouthed little bitch," Austin grunts as he thrusts inside of me, opening me up with a single motion, slicing into me with hot heat and the slam of his hips. I give a wet gasp and run my tongue over my lips, curling up into him and biting at his throat. As soon as my teeth make contact, he's groaning and moving against me harder, rocking his pelvis into mine so hard that I feel like my bones are going to shatter. *And I'd never want them put back together. It would be broken bliss.*

"Austin," I moan, letting myself go. I've learned a very valuable lesson in the past few months: losing yourself makes it easier to find yourself. And if you want to orgasm, you'd best know how to find yourself. Otherwise, you get good sex but no climax. I bend my legs at the knees and spread them as wide as I can, enjoying the feeling of being full, like a puzzle that's just found its missing piece.

"Keep talking to me, babe," he grumbles against my cheek, moving his mouth back to mine and kissing me, even as he roughly pushes my legs apart with one hand and clenches his fingers in my hair with the other. "Keep talkin'. I want to hear your voice."

"Fuck me, Austin," I moan against his mouth, struggling to get the words out between kisses. "Fuck me and ... tell me how good I feel." His tongue slides against mine, hot and hungry while his cock moves inside my pussy, dragging me to the precipice of coming over and over again. Each thrust fills me up another notch, making my body feel itchy and frantic, like it can't happen fast enough. At the same time, I don't want it to happen. I want to keep going, to keep feeling this way forever.

"You're the hottest damn lay I ever had," he snarls into my ear, giving me the chills when his silky hair brushes across my cheek. I doubt he'd like to hear that. I don't think many men strive to achieve *silky* hair, but damn it, he's got it and it's *mine.* "Tighter than any woman I've ever been with." I don't want to hear about other women, not even in the context of my greatness, so I kiss him again, locking my mouth to his while we grind our bodies together. My stomach twists again, but I ignore it. It doesn't matter. Right now, only *this* matters.

"Austin," I cry again, letting him move me closer to climax. "Austin, Austin, Austin." His rhythm speeds up and his body tenses, back muscles clenching as he groans and spills his seed inside of me. I let go of my hold and come, too, trying to match him as he slams into me with a few more, well-placed thrusts. "Austin, I love you."

The words come out, even though I don't mean them, too.

Perhaps ... perhaps fate was involved in this one?

CHAPTER 7

"You look decidedly miserable," Mireya says, slamming her plate down on the table across from me. I don't worry about that – Mireya slams her plate down every day. But today she's actually sitting with me. That's a good sign, isn't it? I sit up straight, sliding my elbow off the table and letting my hand fall into my lap. It's nice to have girlfriends to talk to about man troubles, but what does one do when said girlfriend used to ... well, have *sex* with one's boyfriend?

I focus my gaze on my half-eaten scone and avoid looking at Mireya's frowning face. She's so different than I am. Sometimes if I look at her too hard, I get jealous, just a bit. I was born and bred to be an innocent Southern girl, and I feel like even with these faded jeans and this old T-shirt, I still look like one. Mireya *looks* like a biker. She has this hard edge to her pretty, this sexy flare that I don't think I could ever achieve. She's curvier than I am, and her lips are fuller. I try not to sigh. *Nobody likes a whine, not unless you're serving cheese with it.* Another favorite phrase of my mother.

"It's Austin, isn't it?" she says with a sigh of her own. I look up and follow her red nails as she picks up a piece of toast. We're starting late today. Usually we all get to the house before eight in the morning. I glance up at the clock. It's half past nine already and we're still here having a leisurely breakfast. Or at least some of us are. When I woke up this morning, Austin was already gone. I'm not sure what to think of that. "You might as well just ask me. I've known the asshole for ten years." I lift my eyes up to hers, but she isn't looking at me. She's staring at the tablecloth like it holds all the answers. She seems distant but not upset. Not anymore. Gaine has really transformed Mireya, whether she knows it or not.

Mireya lifts her dark eyes up to mine.

"Well?" I run my suddenly sweaty palms along the fabric of my jeans and take a deep breath, pausing to adjust my ponytail before I speak. This is an awkward moment at best, but I have a feeling that Mireya and I are going to be around one other for a very, very long time. Possibly forever. It might be best if we work through our issues.

"I, um." I bite at my lower lip and reach for my tea. It's ridiculously sugared – like any proper Southern lady's tea should be. "I think I said something to upset Austin last night." I take another sip. "I didn't mean to. It just sort of ... came out."

"During sex?" Mireya asks, absolutely unabashed. Me, I think I blush a bit. I look around at the empty tables, letting my eyes scan the breakfast buffet, before I turn back to Mireya. The last thing I need right now is Gaine or Kimmi or goodness – *Beck* – appearing without my knowledge and overhearing what I'm about to say. I wish I could talk to Christy about this, but she's been skittish when it comes to conversations about sex.

I swallow and adjust myself on the seat, lifting my chin and locking gazes with Mireya.

"I told him I loved him, even though I promised myself that I wouldn't be the first to say it." I blow out a breath and take another sip of my tea. The warm Earl Grey soothes my nerves as I wait for a response. Mireya leans back in her chair, leather jacket crinkling as she purses her red lips and taps her wedding ring against the table. I try not to stare at it, but it's so different from the ones I always saw back home. I swear, there must be some secret committee of women from my church who get together and decide unanimously what rings everyone should wear: 18K white gold with pave-set diamonds, always expensive, but never flashy. Mireya's is actually just the slightest bit rusted with a gleaming red jewel set in the center. I think it may be an actual ruby, but I'm too afraid to ask. It seems so personal somehow.

"What did he do?" she asks me, sounding genuinely interested. I put down my tea cup and pick at my scone again, unearthing small blueberries in the dry dough. *What didn't he do?* is more like the real question. He kissed me, told me I was beautiful, stroked my hair and held me while we fell asleep. He absolutely, one hundred percent did *not* say it back.

"He was as kind and gentlemanly as usual," I say to which Mireya smirks.

"So, not much at all, right?" she asks, and I do my best to smile back since I'm fairly certain it was a joke. "Austin is ... strange. I think he's spent so much of his life running that when it comes time to stand still, he doesn't know what to do anymore. I wouldn't worry about it if I were you." Mireya grits her teeth and then takes a few, deep breaths. I watch in wonder as she visibly relaxes herself. "He's never taken to any woman the way he's taken to you. I'm sure he'll say it back. Just give him time."

"Thank you, Mireya," I say and her smile gets just this much more real, more genuine. What she doesn't know is that I'm only thanking her for her words, not so much for the meaning, because I'm not so sure that she's right. I feel like something is starting to slip inside of Austin, and if I don't find it soon, he may very well find himself in a crisis of character.

CHAPTER 8

Austin

Melissa looks ten years younger – I kid you not. I swear, some of the lines in her face have disappeared, and she's back to her old self, hanging on Tax and swinging her blonde hair around like she doesn't have a care in the world. I hope she takes her vows of holy matrimony more seriously this time than she did the first round. Not that I suppose I can truly hold it against her. Kent Diamond wasn't the nicest man to have ever graced this here fine earth.

"Thank you for allowing us free passage through your territory," Tax says formally, holding out his hand for me to shake. I reach out and grab it firmly, giving him a nod as I step back into line with Beck. Right now, it's just me, him, and three other Triple M'ers. I left everybody else at the hotel with instructions not to show up before eleven. We got shit to take care of here first.

Don't think about Amy, I warn myself as my mind starts to wander again. How could I not though? *She said she loved your pathetic fucking ass last night and what did you do besides shit your damn pants in fear?* Fuck almighty. I really am a stupid Goddamn man.

"Thank you for letting us get the opportunity to spend time with your sister. Tease is an incredible person," I say, hoping that Beck doesn't make any rude ass comments. I give him a sidelong glance, but he doesn't return it, keeping his attention fully focused on Tax's face. Surprisingly, he doesn't even bother to look over at Melissa. The man returns his stare, green eyes blazing in the hot glare of the sun. I feel like there's something they both know that I don't. It's makin' me uncomfortable.

"If you ever hurt her, I will kill you. You have my word." Tax doesn't look at me when he says this, but I get the idea that the entire group is implicated in his statement. He blinks his eyes a few times and touches a hand to his red hair, sweeping some strands away from his face. "Now, where the fuck are our little friends?"

I turn around and survey the empty street, but it's dead as a desert out here, and I ain't got any answers for him.

"They heard your name and they ran like little bitches, scurryin' off into the sunset." Beck grins, flashing his white teeth as he turns and looks at the small group behind us. I've never been all that good with makin' my rounds in the group, but I take note of the faces and try to place names. *Joel, Bishop, and Bryan.* All three of them joined Triple M after me, but they've still been around a long while. I try to pony up a slight smile. This President shit is one of the hardest damn things I've ever done.

"If they're not here," Tax says, glancing back at his boys. "Then we're just going to have to find them." I watch as he pulls out a phone and disappears into the mass of bikes at his back, weaving between metal frames with ease. His men stare at us with neutral expressions, but I get the distinct impression that were we to lift a single fuckin' finger towards them, they'd shoot us all dead. I took a big gamble by coming out here to meet them, but at least for now, it looks like it's going to pay off.

Melissa gives us a tight smile and follows after Tax. I watch her go and then turn around and move towards the house. When Tax is done doing whatever he's doing, I'm sure he'll send someone to come get me. Might as well take a moment to look inside while I wait.

My Triple M'ers follow after me, waiting on the walkway as I unlock the door and move inside. The house is hotter than a submarine in the center of the sun, and I ain't got patience for that. *Air conditioning just moved to the top of my list.*

"Hey Boss," Beck drawls, moving up beside me. He trails after me as I head to the back door and slide it open, lighting a cigarette and glancing over my shoulder at him. "Can I talk to you for a minute?" I shrug and look back at the other guys, giving them a nod that I hope means *leave us the hell alone for a second.* I step outside and Beck follows.

"What is it, Evans?" I ask him as I smoke my cigarette and try to calm the uncertainty inside my gut. I don't like feeling like this. It took me a little while to explain it, to understand the fear that's roiling there like a summer storm, but I get it now. *What if I'm not good enough?* The question keeps coming up in my mind, playin' on repeat, and I can't shake the feeling that the answer is, *you aren't. You aren't ready to be President, Sparks. You aren't ready to lead these people. Look at what you gone and done so far? You got ten of your members murdered. They're dead, Austin, and they ain't never coming back.*

And then there's Amy. Oh, Christ on a fucking cracker. Amy.

I don't know how to be a partner. I've never been with a single woman like this before. This is the only time in my damn life I've ever been monogamous, and it's the first time anyone's ever said *I love you* to me when I've actually wanted to say it back. So what do I do now? How do I get through this when all I feel like I'm doing is failing?

"I want to tell you somethin'." Beck holds up his hands. "It's good news though, so no worryin'." He pauses to clear his throat and adjust his stupid T-shirt. Another tight one, like he's in a fucking rock band or something. He tries not to smile, but the expression cracks through his face like we was born with it. I bet he came out of his momma, grinnin' away like an idiot. "Tease is pregnant."

I drop my cigarette to the grass and watch as Beck's red brows rise up in surprise.

"It ain't a ghost, Sparks. Don't look so damn scared." He crushes the smoldering cig out with his boot before it catches the brown grass on fire. "This is a good thing. Good timing, too." Beck gestures up at the clubhouse. "We get to all co-exist like a happy fuckin' family." My throat goes dry, and I end up sitting down on one of the old lawn chairs. I don't know why I'm freaking out so damn much. To be honest, if my friend is happy, then I'm happy. But ... shit. It might not be my baby – God knows what I'd do if it were – but it feels like another load of responsibility has just been heaped up on my shoulders, and I'm staggering under the weight.

"I'm real happy for you, Beck," I tell him, trying to get across some genuine feeling in my tone. Something other than fear, that is. My friend puts his big hands on his hips and stares me down. I do my best not to meet his gaze.

"Austin Sparks, if I didn't know any better, I'd think you'd just been shot straight through the chest. Come on now, this is something to celebrate. If I'd have known you were going to freak out, I woulda waited for a better moment."

"I'm alright. Really, I'm happy for you, Beck. I just … this whole thing with Broken Dallas is startin' to get on my nerves." I force myself to my feet, and give my friend a hug. The last thing I want to do right now is ruin his moment. "You tell Gaine or Kimmi yet?" Beck shrugs and lights up a cigarette of his own.

"Kimmi, yeah. Not Gaine." He grins wider. "You see, I got a peckin' order for y'all that I like to stick to. Besides," Beck glances up at the house, "Gaine'll get all gushy and excited on me. I want to save that shit for last." He moves towards the stairs and I follow, just in time to intercept a man from Seventy-seven Brothers.

Is it a bad sign that I'm almost *relieved* to go back to dealing with this shit? Violence is one thing, but babies? Shit. I don't know anything about that.

The man doesn't say anything, just gestures for us to follow him back outside where Tax is waiting. When he turns around to look at us, I see that he's frowning deeply.

"Couldn't find 'em?" I ask before he gets a chance to speak.

"Actually," Tax says, removing a pistol from the holster at his side. "We did. And it's time to intact retribution for crimes committed."

CHAPTER 9

When we arrive at the house, I climb off my bike – yes, yes, *yes*, I rode it here all by myself – and head inside to start work. Yesterday was girls' day off; tomorrow is boys' day off. Today, we all work together. Except for Austin, Beck, and a few of the others. I try not to think too hard about the message Kimmi received before we got here. *They're chasing after Broken Dallas.* My stomach turns, and I clutch a hand to my mouth. *I think I'm going to be sick.*

"Are you alright?" Tease asks me, tilting her head to the side and studying me with narrowed green eyes. Her red hair frames her porcelain skin like rubies. Where I'm your plain, average, American white girl, Tease is not. She's one of those women that once you catch sight of them, you can't look away. She's pretty in a different way than Mireya but just as fierce. "Because you don't look it."

I start to mumble that I'm fine, but my stomach turns again, and I end up in the downstairs bathroom, puking in a most unladylike manner. Lucky for me, I also get an audience to view my shame.

"What's wrong?" Kimmi asks, crowding her red head in next to Tease's. "Did you eat the scrambled eggs this morning? I ate the scrambled eggs, and I'm not feeling too hot myself. I think they were undercooked."

"Could I please have a moment?" I ask, trying not to sound exasperated. Another wave of nausea hits me as I grip the rim of the dirty toilet seat. We took down the hideous ceiling tiles in this room yesterday, and the whole thing is covered in dust and grit. Just thinking of it makes me throw up again.

"Do you need me to get you anything?" Christy asks as I sit back and wipe my mouth with some spare toilet paper. I look up into her blue eyes, taking solace in the cool calmness of them. She's most at home here in the soon-to-be clubhouse I've noticed. Christy might be 'afraid' of motorcycles, but she's certainly not afraid of home renovations. I saw her dive into the kitchen demo with a ferocity that was nearly frightening.

"Some water, if you could, please?" I ask, leaning

against the wall and crossing one arm over my belly. When Christy returns with my drink, I grab her hand and pull her down to sit beside me, making certain that the toilet is flushed and the seat down first, thank you very much. "I think I'll sit for awhile," I tell her as she settles in with her back against the corner vanity. It's a tiny, dinky thing with a brass faucet and an avocado green countertop that most likely was put in at least a decade before I was even born. "Keep me company?" Christy nods and scoops her hair up, putting the blonde strands into a ponytail with a band she's got around her wrist. Her neck looks long and pale, like a swan's. "We don't get to spend as much time together as I'd like," I admit, and she smiles.

"You're busy," she says and then blushes. "Crap." Christy's delicate hands fly up to her mouth and her eyes go wide. She draws them away slowly. "Shit," she whispers, and her smile returns with a vengeance. I grin back.

"Damn it," I growl, leaning a bit closer. But not too close. Some teeth brushing might be in order before that happens.

"Bitch," she says a little louder.

"Hell. Bastard. Tits. Ass." I wave my hands around and then cup them over my mouth. "Fuck!" I scream, letting the word echo around the enclosed space.

"Pussy, taint, cunt," Christy shouts back, and we descend into fits of laughter. It's a bit childish, but you try living your whole life with the threat of soap in your mouth and see how you do. Honestly, my mother would put whole bars of Dove down my throat and make me sit with them for an hour. Then, of course, my father would come home and it wouldn't be enough. I'd get the belt and be sent to bed without dinner. For saying *shit*. It only ever happened twice, but I wasn't eager to repeat it. This newfound freedom we've discovered is quite exhilarating.

"Now, what on earth is going on in here?" Kimmi asks, sliding into view. Her emerald earrings sway with her movement. Most of us – including Mireya – put on jeans and T-shirts for the renovation work. Not Kimmi. She shows up in the same sorts of outfits she always wears: high heeled boots, tight leather pants, and usually a corset or bedazzled tank top of some sort. Today she's got on a green top that matches her earrings, with little silver beads sewn into it. Her pants are black, tight, and made of leather as per usual, but today she's switched it up a bit with some purple sequined heels. I guess if you can rob banks and outrun the cops in stilettos, you can certainly knock down a wall or two.

I pretend not to notice as Christy's eyes take her all in, and a blush rises on her cheeks.

"I distinctly heard the word *pussy*, so I had to make sure there wasn't a party I was missing out on." Kimmi winks her long eyelashes, honing her gaze on Christy with laser focus. I clear my throat and glance at the ugly diamond patterned wallpaper near my face. "Hey, Christy, I was thinking that if you wanted, we could take my bike out tonight, and I could give you some tips on riding." My friend's eyes go wide and she switches her gaze over to me. I pretend to be interested in the wallpaper. "It's a nice night for it, so … "

"I'll think about it," Christy chirps, standing up so quickly that she stumbles and ends up in Kimmi's arms, sort of like something you'd see in a romantic comedy. I pick at the peeling wallpaper with my nails, and force back another wave of nausea. It would not do to go vomiting during my friend's special moment. The two of them are caught, looking into one another's eyes. First love is a beautiful, beautiful thing, isn't it? I wonder if Christy knows she's got a crush yet.

"I'll ask again later," Kimmi says, letting go of Christy and taking a step back. She glances sidelong down the hallway, and a crooked smile lights her pink tinged lips. "Maybe after lunch?" And then she winks at Christy and disappears. My friend brushes her hands on her new jeans (possibly the first pair she's ever owned) and walks out of the bathroom with her head held high, just in time for me to grab another private moment to puke.

When I come out, most of the work is in full swing. There are a few Triple M'ers smoking cigarettes and drinking beer in the backyard, but I know they'll get around to it. Never in my life have a met such a hardworking group of people. I smile and resist the urge to go fetch my book out of my saddlebags. The day before yesterday, Austin caught me sneaking a chapter in the upstairs bathroom and made fun of me all day. One of these days, I'm going to convince him to read a book. I've already manged to rope Mireya, Kimmi, and even Melissa into trying one of my Sali Bend novels. It's just a matter of time.

I head up the stairs, running my hand along the freshly painted banister. It gleams a pearly white in the early afternoon sun. I give it a friendly pat and pause on the landing, trying to remember which of the rooms are already painted. I catch Christy in the third room on my right, a roller in hand, and join her. Not to be rude or anything, but some of these bikers have a sloppy hand when it comes to painting, so Christy and I have taken over. And besides, we're a little less capable of picking up a set of cabinets and moving them single-handedly. Some of the folks here have biceps the size of my thigh for goodness sake.

I pick up a paint brush and dip it into the can, enjoying the smooth texture of the wet paint. The color we've chosen for this room is a frosty green, like mint chocolate chip ice cream. Supposedly, this is going to be Gaine and Mireya's room.

"Amy, is there anything you want to tell me?" Christy asks which I know is code for *there's something I want to tell* you, *so please, give me something in return.* It's much easier to spill a secret when someone's already given you one. I smile at her and move over to the window, carefully painting the spots around the white trim. My stomach is still a tad uneasy, but I don't think too hard about it.

"Like what?" I ask, struggling to keep my eyes on the paint job and off the deserted neighborhood out the window. This window faces West, and I can only imagine that there are going to be some spectacular sunsets to be seen from this vantage point. I pause, spotting movement in the bushes a couple of houses down. *Cat?* I wonder. *Or maybe dog?* I'd like to get a dog eventually. A small one. One that I can take on my bike with me. I smile as I get a more modern version of Dorothy and Toto in my head. *How silly is that?*

"You know, just whatever," she says, trying desperately to sound nonchalant. I sweep the brush down the wall and turn around, splattering a tiny bit of paint on the brown paper covering the floor. Christy is blushing, redness spreading down her neck and across her bare shoulders. I let my lips twitch into a smile as I re-dip my brush and turn back towards the window to paint. My guess is that she's going to admit she has a thing for Kimmi. I expect us to break down into a giggling fit of girlishness.

I certainly don't expect the gunshot.

One moment, I'm painting the wall and humming *Do You Believe in Magic* by The Lovin' Spoonful, and the next, the brush is clattering to the floor and I'm clutching my arm. The window in front of me drops into pieces, falling like rain to my feet. I realize that it probably shattered *before* I was shot, but things are so blurry in my mind that this is how I remember it later.

I scream, and press my fingers so tight to the wound that redness oozes between them, sliding down my skin in hot heat and splattering on the floor next to my paint dribbles.

"Amy!" Christy screeches as I stumble to the side and slam my back into the partially wet wall.

"Get down!" I shout at my friend. "On the floor!" I slide down as Christy drops her roller and falls to her knees. Literally, seconds later, there are sounds of shouting outside and in. Some of the girls appear in the doorway, ducking low and skittering across the floor towards me.

"Let me see it!" Kimmi says, reaching out and trying to pry my hands away. I bite my lower lip and close my eyes, fighting the wave of overwhelming nausea and vertigo that's gripped me. *I've been shot.* It's a surreal thought, to be sure. *I wonder what Mother would say?* I release my fingers and groan as a wave of biting pain cuts through my arm and swirls straight up to my brain.

"Here," Tease says, passing over a clean rag and kneeling down next to Kimmi. Christy crawls up beside her and presses her back against the wall next to me. Her blue eyes are wide with fear and dripping with tears.

"I'm okay. I'm alright." I keep repeating the words, trying to move my hand over to grasp my friend's. My arm refuses to heed my demands and stays stone still while Kimmi and Tease fuss over it. "I'm fine. I'll be okay."

"You're in shock is what you are," Kimmi growls, rising up on her knees and peering outside. I turn my head to look and the world spins. I see Triple M'ers in the streets with guns and wrenches and hammers, but I don't hear anymore shots. *What happened? Who shot me*? I wonder as my head lolls on my shoulders and my chin comes to rest on my chest. "You're lucky," Kimmi breathes, tying the rag around my arm. "It went straight through." She looks over her shoulder and stares at the bullet hole in the other wall.

"Who functions as your medic?" Tease asks, scooting over and pushing Christy out of the way, so she can help me up. I groan as Kimmi and Tease heft me up on their shoulders.

"Medic? She needs to get to a hospital!" Christy shouts, stumbling after us as we move out of the room and into the hallway. I focus on the droplets of blood that hit the floor and think absently that they look like the ruby on Mireya's ring.

"Hospitals ask too many questions," Tease says before Kimmi gets a chance to answer her. "Club business should stay club business."

"We've got Didi," Kimmi says as we start down the stairs. "This wouldn't be the first time she's patched up a gunshot. It'll be alright. You got lucky, babe. It could've been a hell of a lot worse."

Tease and Kimmi take me out back and put me in one of the lawn chairs, setting me down gently. Tease stays behind and covers me with her jacket while Kimmi disappears to find Didi. Christy kneels down in the grass beside me, tears streaming down her face.

"I promise, I'm going to make it through just fine," I say, trying to calm her down a bit. I feel so strange. The pain has subsided, and the world is fuzzy around the edges. Shock. Yes, I think I'm most certainly in it. I know it's dangerous, but that's about as far as my knowledge extends. Hopefully this Didi will know a bit more than I do.

"Fucking fuckers!" Mireya snarls as she appears in the doorway, coming down the steps with an older woman at her heels. I've been trying my best to remember everyone's faces and names, but I don't know who this is. I imagine she must be Didi.

"Let's see it," she says, getting down to business by dropping what looks like a toolbox near my feet.

"Did you see who did it?" Kimmi asks, coming back out of the house and pausing with her phone resting in her hand. Her brows are pinched together and her lips turned down in a rare frown. My gaze gets caught on her earrings and can't seem to move away from the glittering green spots. Whiteness eats at the edges of my vision, threatening to knock me out, but I fight against it, struggling to stay awake.

"Nobody did. We thought it might be Broken Dallas or something, but there's no one out there that we can see. God-fucking-damn it." Mireya spins in a nervous circle and pauses with her attention on the phone in

Kimmi's hand. "You didn't text Austin yet, did you?" she asks as Gaine comes out the back doors.

"There's nothing," he says, spitting at the dirt and pausing with his hands on his hips. "No sign of anybody out there." He raises his face up and looks at me, skin paling when he sees the redness oozing from my arm. Didi removes the rag and tosses it to the grass, opening her kit and digging around inside. I close my eyes and look away. If I look at whatever she's doing, I'll pass out for sure.

"Enough jaw flappin'," the old woman barks, her voice as rough as leather. "Grab me a pen and some paper. I'm going to make you a list of stuff to go get. And make it quick. We ain't got all day." I listen to Gaine's footsteps as he moves away at a rapid pace.

"Don't tell Austin or he'll freak the fuck out and run back here. We don't know what he's up to, and we can't risk distracting him."

"I got it, Mireya. Geez." I open my eyes and look up to see Kimmi putting away her phone. She glances at Didi and moves a few steps closer, leaning down to peer at the wound again. I keep my gaze averted.

"Got the list," Gaine says, reappearing and handing it to Didi who scribbles a few things down and thrusts it at his chest.

"Quick, Gaine," she tells him, and he nods, heading

out the back gate. A few seconds later, I hear the sound of a motorcycle starting up.

"Get ready for this, girl," Didi says, and I make the mistake of looking back at her, finding a curved needle in her calloused hand.

I swallow hard and hear Christy say, "Oh my God. You're not planning on stabbing her with that, are you?" That's the last thing I remember before I pass out.

CHAPTER 10
Austin

I've got my new Ruger P95 pistol in my hands. It feels nice and sturdy, like I could take down a Goddamn bear with it. Good thing, too, because some of these boys in Broken Dallas are the size of grizzlies.

"This is fucking bullshit," Beck grumbles under his breath, taking aim with fingers quivering with adrenaline. "Hiding back here like a bunch of pussycats. What does Tax take us for, huh?"

"I think he realizes you're the guy that just banged his sister," I say, and I hear a bunch of gruff chuckles from the three Triple M'ers standing beside us. "So shut your damn mouth and just be glad he hasn't castrated you yet. We're along on this expedition as guests, Beck. Be grateful Seventy-seven Brothers even bothered to ride down here. If they hadn't, we'd have been up shit creek without a paddle."

"Hogwash. I coulda took 'em," Beck says with a grin, taking a peek around the corner. I scoot closer and take a look, too. Tax is nowhere to be seen, but his new Sergeant at arms is standing at the head of the group, hands crossed in front of him. I can't hear what they're saying, but the look on Mr. Silver Beard's face ain't pleasant.

The sun is shining and everything seems all hunky-dory on the surface of things. I have no idea where we are or why we're here, but there's nobody around to complain. We're in a warehouse district, one that's conspicuously empty on this bright sunny day. I don't pretend to know what Broken Dallas is up to, but it seems a little weird, even considering the bad blood between us.

I stay where I am, waiting for this to end with a bunch of posturing and some grunts of acknowledgment. I don't expect violence, not today. That's not the way these things usually go, not at first. But as I'm standing there and watching the wind blow the weeds at my feet, a shot explodes and blood splatters the pavement near the Sergeant's feet. Silver Beard crumples to the cement like a broken doll.

An instant later, the street descends into chaos.

"Hell yeah!" Beck shouts, and I damn hear shoot *him* in the back when he takes off runnin', heading straight for the action.

"Son of a bitch," I growl under my breath, reaching around the corner and taking aim. I am so sick of firefights, I could spit. "Mother fucker. Baby Jesus give me strength." I shoot a man in the thigh when he gets close and nearly jump out of my fuckin' skin when a shot goes off behind me. I spin to find a couple of guys behind us, holding guns and wearing colors that I know all too well. Bested by Crows. When the shit hits the fan, it just splatters, don't it?

I drop to my knee and miss getting shot in the face by a margin so small, it makes my dead grandma sweat in her grave. I take aim at the first man, a guy with bright blonde hair and a face that makes me think maybe he's related to the late Walker brothers. *Good riddance*, I think as I shoot him right in the chest. No playing around. I don't like to kill, but if it's me or them, then shit, it's going to be them.

My man drops just a split second before the other two do. I glance over at my boys with a determined set to my lips, not quite a smile, not quite a frown.

"Don't get killed, alright?" I ask, rising to my feet and swinging around the side of the building. I hear a small chorus of *yes, Pres* as I move low to the ground, pausing behind one of Seventy-seven Brothers' bikes. I keep my gun raised and pull my phone out with my other hand, shooting off a text to Tax. He might not get it, but I ain't got a damn clue where he is and somebody needs to know that Bested by Crows is here, too.

Beck is standing straight up, his red hair bright under the sunlight. There's a bit of blood on his lip and a crumpled man at his feet, but otherwise he looks okay to me. I put my phone away and sit up, looking out at a suddenly silent battleground. This doesn't descend into hand-to-hand combat like it did in Korbin when we were fighting Seventy-seven Brothers. Everybody but Beck has taken cover, and all I can see are bikes and bodies.

"Where's that bitch, Margot Tempe?" I hear a voice ask from the front, somebody from our side. "She rightfully belongs to us. Hand her over and accept retribution for the crimes committed against the Brothers. You do that, and we're gone, headed back home."

Nobody bothers to answer.

The silence stretches long and tight while we wait in tense anticipation.

I happen to glance over and find Melissa smiling at me from behind a nearby bike. I can't even believe Tax let her out here to fight. I shake my head. What am I sayin'? Let her? Nobody *lets* or doesn't let this woman do a damn thing. She goes about life as she pleases.

"Who's askin' after my ol' lady?" one of the men says, rising to his feet. He's got dark hair and dark eyes, a goatee, and a bad case of overconfidence. He stands out in the open, the perfect target, but nobody shoots him. There's a Code of the Road here, and I know I ain't the only one that believes in it. They *might* shoot this dude in the head, but they'll wait until after this conversation is over. *Fuck my stars.*

"I am."

Tax appears on the top of a nearby building. I get the impression that he's not often seen in public. I know I'm a bit different than most MC Presidents. Usually, you don't see the fuckers. Who puts their leader in harm's way? But my group is small, and this is how we've always done things, so it's the way it's gonna stay. Besides, I'm not the type to sit back and wait.

"Turn her over to us for crimes committed. I count nine of yours dead, including your Sergeant at arms. I'll take that as retribution. Now, hand over Margot and our business is finished here. We're done." Tax slaps his palms together, dusting them off and holding them open wide. It seems like as fair an offer as anyone's going to get in this situation, and the guy with the goatee looks like he's considering it. *Looks* bein' the key word, I guess.

Another shot rings out and one of Tax's men shoves him out of the way only to get hit in the shoulder. His body pinwheels over the edge of the building, and it's like a switch has been flicked. More Bested by Crows members spill out from behind the chain link fence at our right, leaving bleeding bodies where Seventy-seven Brothers' sentries were stationed.

"Shit a bitch," I growl, rising to my feet and holstering my gun, switching it out for the crowbar I stuffed down the back of my damn pants. I hear Beck's battle whoop a split second before my ears go dumb from the sound of so many guns going off around me. Bullets whiz by, but I don't pay 'em much nevermind. Beck's a Goddamn battle axe, but I'm a limber son of a bitch. I don't have to pull any *Matrix* shit though because these guys are here with a different purpose – to disarm us motherfuckers.

I slam my crowbar into the arm of the first guy that charges me. Call me a pussy if you want, but I don't exactly enjoy the feeling of a weapon crushing a man's skull. I leave that shit to Beck Evans.

Or to Melissa Diamond.

I wonder if she's changed her name? I think as she takes a baseball bat and swings it for a home run. The man I attacked collapses to his knees, bending low with blood streaming down the sides of his face. Melissa doesn't let it end there, and I force myself to turn away. Don't need to see that shit. I push through the crowd, hitting guys out of the way as I go. I'm not exactly a martial arts expert, so I won't be missed much in the melee of things. What I can do is take a wild guess on what's going on here.

I manage to make it to the back of the crowd, moving into an empty space in the back gravel of the parking lot. I look around quickly, trying to get a lay of the land so to speak.

"Where'd they come from?" Tax asks, showing up at my side with a half-dozen guys.

"I'm not sure," I say, leading the way and ducking under the chain link fence. Tax and his guys follow me, moving across the pavement at a low run. When we come around the corner of a rusted outbuilding, we run into a group of guys I didn't expect.

With motherfucking *machine guns*.

"Holy shit." I draw back before they see me and hold out my arm to stop Tax from moving forward. "Holy shit," I whisper, thinking maybe I underestimated the situation a bit. My guess was that there were some guys waiting in the wings, getting ready to flank us or some shit. What I didn't expect were Goddamn *machine guns.* I ain't no gun expert, but I think they're M16s.

I gesture back at the fence, and move without waiting to see if Tax is following. I have no plans on getting ripped full of bullet holes. *Son of a bitch.*

"What?" Tax demands as soon as we're on the other side of the fence, backs pressed against the brick building where I started just a few, agonizing minutes ago. When I thought we might escape without violence. What a fuckin' crock.

"There's a group of guys back there with M16s," I snap at him, wiping sweat from my forehead. I glance around the corner and notice that the tide has turned. The Bested by Crows members have subtly moved the fight back towards Broken Dallas. Fucking genius. I don't have to tell Tax what I'm thinking. *They're going to slaughter us. All of us. Code of the Road? What the fuck was I thinking?*

"We need to get out of here," I tell Tax, but he's already moving away from me. "Where the fuck are you going?" I growl at him, following after his back. He moves around the fence, keeping his voice low when he responds.

"Taking care of business," he snaps.

My lip curls, but I stay with him, wondering if maybe I might learn something. Tax has been President for awhile now, and I've only ever heard impressive things about Seventy-seven Brothers.

We move around the fence, pausing right about where the men with the fucking machine guns were standing. Tax moves slowly towards the fence and pauses to peek through. I don't know how much he can see. This shit ain't chain link, and the wood is solid. I move up beside him and take a look for myself. The men aren't moving, just standing there. I have no fucking clue what they're waiting for. From what I figure, if they moved in now, they'd have a pretty solid chance of taking out all of Seventy-seven Brothers' men with a few well-placed presses on those triggers. I can't know for sure, but I get the idea that these aren't semi-automatics. I reckon these motherfuckers got theyselves some automatic weapons. Legality ain't an issue here. If it were, we'd all be stock brokers or bank tellers.

I could be wrong, of course. Maybe I'm overreacting? But shoot, then why the hell are these assholes standing around here? Why the fancy ass weapons?

"Is this a massacre?" Tax whispers, stepping back and looking around. It's odd how similar to Tease he is. Same hair, same eyes, same nose. If he wasn't a decade or more older than her, I might think they were twins. Despite everything that's happened, he seems like a good man. "Well, if that's the plan, we're going to change fate."

We all pause to listen, out of habit I think, but the only sounds are the sounds of battle on the street one over from us. No sirens. Huh.

I sneak another peek through the fence and try to count the number of guys waiting back there, perfectly still, taut with tension. *What the fuck are they waiting for?* I don't know how good of an idea it is to wait around and find out.

Amy pops into my head, almost randomly, and I start thinking again about what would happen if I died here today. It's a morbid train of thought that I push back, trying to think only of her perfect face, her sweet lips, her beautiful body. I squeeze my hands into tight fists by my sides. I'd give anything to be back at our clubhouse, paintin' walls and shit, but this is the crap I have to deal with. That I might always have to deal with. *I should've let Kent live*, I think which is a stupid thought. This is all his fucking fault in the first place. We had a sweet deal going on before.

I try to tell myself I can do this, but it isn't easy. It's hard to march on when you feel inadequate in every Goddamn way possible. Tax is the type of man I should be, but I'm not.

I look around the alley we're standing in and spot a

dumpster near the exit to the street. And then I get an idea. It's not a very brilliant one, but I don't see what other choice we got.

"Come on," I whisper, moving ahead of Tax and his men, pausing next to the rusted green piece of crap and trying to figure out the best way to climb up.

"What the fuck are you doing?" Tax asks. I feel like he's *this* damn close to charging in there and trying to take those assholes on with his bare hands. I doubt he'd actually go through with it, but it makes me feel better that I have plan that's at least one step away from that desperation. Fuck, maybe we're overreacting anyway, and these guys are just back up? I don't know. But I don't like the way this is looking.

I move around the dumpster and use the building next to it to push my way up, muscles straining as I try to stay silent. I slide up on my belly and scoot across the lid until I'm as close to the fence as possible. If someone were to look this way right now, they might see a hint of my fat ass sticking up above the fence, but fortunately, their attention is on the battle that's still taking place.

Without my having to ask, Tax and his men copy me, moving up alongside my frozen form. It only takes them a minute. Good thing, too, because as soon as we're in place, the men turn and start to move towards the chain link fence. I don't know what the signal was, but there they go, off and runnin'.

"Ready," I say, glancing down the line. I get a nod from Tax as I pull my Ruger out and hold it tight in my sweaty fingers. "Now!" I whisper harshly, and the eight of us rise to our knees, take aim, and fire.

CHAPTER 11
Austin

By the time I get back to the clubhouse, I am a fucking wreck. I've shed more blood today than I have in the rest of my life combined. I don't much like the feeling. At least I got my boys by my side still. Didn't lose a single member of Triple M. I didn't ask how many Seventy-seven Brothers lost – it wasn't my place.

"Lights are still on," Beck says cheerfully as we pause in the driveway and I get off to open the garage door. There are a lot of bikes in here, not the whole club obviously, but a few. Beck and I park, leaving the guys to clean 'em up. Blood fucks up the paint job, you know.

I sweep a hand though my hair and exchange a look with Beck. I don't really know how to describe what happened today. A fucking nightmare. That's what it was. At least Tax and I got that shit taken care of. Thing is, I don't know that we're done. I don't know that this is over. We didn't kill everyone, obviously. A couple of minutes after we got back to the fight, Broken Dallas and Bested by Crows started looking worried and fled. We didn't bother to give chase. It was rough enough as is. And then I spent the last few hours treating the wounded and moving the dead. Fucking hell. I don't ever want to do that shit again.

"Keep the details to yourself for a little while," I tell Beck as we open the front door and come in to find an empty entryway. There were a few guys out front, but they didn't say anything when I came in, just nodded to acknowledge me. A quick glance out the back windows shows me that there a bunch of Triple M'ers in the yard with a fire going, drinking beer and having a good time. I don't know if they realize how serious this crap is.

"I got a bad feeling in my stomach, Beck," I tell him as we pause on our way to the back door and glance up. Kimmi's standing at the top of the stairs looking nervous. I don't like nervous. Scares the everliving crap out of me. I grit my teeth hard and turn towards her. "What is it now?" I ask, stretched thin, tired, pissed the fuck off. When she speaks, my heart nearly explodes inside my chest.

"It's Amy."

I'm up the stairs before she can utter another word, headed straight down the hall towards the only bedroom that's lit up. The door slams into the wall when I shove my way through and find Amy resting on a cot in the corner. Her friend Christy is asleep on a lawn chair nearby while Tease watches over them, a book clutched in her hands as she lounges on the end of the cot. My heart is thumping so loud I can barely hear my own words when they come tumbling out of my mouth.

"What happened?" I whisper as Beck and Kimmi move into the room behind me and pause. It feels like there's a sea of tension between me and Amy, like a laser focus aimed at those big, blue eyes. If anyone crosses my path, it's cuttin' em down.

"Oh, Austin," Amy chirps, trying to sound cheerful. I must have a God-awful look on my face. "I'm glad you're back." Her voice quivers briefly before she gathers herself together and unconsciously crosses an arm across her chest, fingers coming to rest on a bandage on the opposite side.

"What happened?" I ask again, but nobody seems to want to answer me. I don't know if they're scared of me or what, but lips stay sealed and gazes travel elsewhere around the room.

"I was going to call or text you, but Mireya made a good point," Kimmi begins as I start across the room, boots loud on the covered wood floors. Amy watches me come, raising her chin, face stoic. "We thought you might be in a sticky situation, and we didn't want to distract you."

I lean down and cup a hand gently against the back of Amy's head, pressing my lips against hers. I don't realize that I'm the one trembling until I pull back and glance down at my hands.

"Somebody took a shot through one of the windows on the West side of the house," Tease says, scooting off the bed and shivering when Beck comes up behind her and wraps an arm around her waist. "Amy got hit in the arm. It's a clean wound though," she adds, like that even matters to me. *Somebody shot my Amy? Somebody fucking shot her?* My vision flickers darkly for a moment, and I glance over my shoulder.

"Get out."

"Austin," Kimmi begins, but I turn my head and give her a look, too. She raises both hands, purses her lips and then shakes her head. "Never mind then. Christy?" Amy's friend rises to her feet, puts a hand on Amy's shoulder as if asking permission. Amy nods at her and she pulls away, taking Beck and Tease along with her. I put my forehead against Amy's uninjured arm and breath in, out, in again.

"I survived a gunshot," Amy says, reaching her fingers of her good hand up to play with my hair. "I assume this gives me some sort of street cred?" she asks, and I chuckle softly, keeping my head down. I feel like fucking shit. There should be some sort of high from coming out on top today, some sort of relief from finding out that Amy's alright, that it's not as serious as it could've been. Instead, all I feel is darkness inside of me. My mind flutters through images, moments in life that I'd rather not relive. Like my brother. How I got him shot. But he wasn't as lucky as Amy.

I look up and find a worried face and flat lips. Amy's brows are pinched together as she waits for me to say something. I sit up a bit and perch on the edge of the cot, listening to the squeak of the springs with gritted teeth. She shouldn't be laying here on this old piece of shit. I want Amy to have a good life, an easy one. Because I love her. I do. I figured that shit out, back when I saw Kent trying to kill her, when there was red oozing down her tender throat. I open my mouth to say the words, but they get stuck inside, frozen there along with my heart.

"This is my fault, sugar," I say. "And I'm sorry. I'm so, so sorry." I shake my head and get out a cigarette, lighting up and rising to my feet to open the window and waft the smoke out the screen. If I sit near her a moment longer, I'm going to crack. Amy watches me, resting her head back into the pillows and running her fingers of her left hand across the cover of a book. The girl is always reading, always lost inside a book. I asked her once, a few weeks back, if reading was an escape. You know what she said? *It used to be, but now, now it's just a vacation.* I ain't got the slightest idea what that means, but it almost made me curious enough to find out.

"Did you pull the trigger?" Amy asks, and I can already see where this is going. I turn back to her, watching the soft fall of chestnut hair around her gorgeous face. She adjusts herself and the blankets fall down her chest, exposing a hint of cleavage above the line of her tank top. I try not to look at it, but fuck. I want to toss my cigarette to the floor, storm across the room in a flurry of unfettered emotions, and kiss the ever livin' crap out of her. Then I want to rip those blankets the rest of the way off, strip her and kiss her entire body before I make sweet motherfucking love to her.

But I don't do any of that.

First off, because the girl's been frigging shot, and second, I have the answer to my question. I am *not* good enough for this woman. If I was, I wouldn't be dragging her through this shit. Getting shot at is nothing compared to what could happen. If what I saw today is any indication, we're all in a heap of shit.

"That shouldn't have ever happened to you, Cross," I say, letting my gaze take in the orange spots of the streetlights. "I should never have dragged you into this shit."

Amy turns and puts her feet on the ground, mouth downturned and face flushed.

"What the hell you doin', sugar?" I ask, crushing my cigarette out in the glass ashtray that's sitting on the windowsill. I move over to her, but she stands up, steady on her feet.

"What do you mean by that?" she asks, and I glance away. I don't know if it's the day I've had or just everything catching up to me all at once, but suddenly I feel antsy. Like I need to ride. Just take off into the night with no idea of where I'm going. *I'm a fucking wimp. Jesus, where the hell did my balls go?*

"I mean I should've left you back in that little town of yours." As soon as I say the words, I know they don't sound the way I meant them to. Amy slaps me across the face, not hard, just enough to let me know that I'm not wanted in here right now. All I want to do is hold her tight, but instead, I find myself backing towards the door.

"Go find yourself again, Austin Sparks, and then come back and see me in the morning." Amy turns back around and climbs into bed, lying on her back with an arm flung over her face. I turn the light off on the way out and don't look back.

CHAPTER 12
AMY

I spend the night at the clubhouse with some of the Triple M'ers and wake feeling sore and slightly dizzy but okay. *I think I'll survive this,* I tell myself with a smile, pausing in the freshly remodeled bathroom that adjoins my room. *Our* room, I correct myself. This corner room I've just spent the last few hours tossing and turning in is supposed to belong to me and Austin.

I mean I should've left you back in that little town of yours.

I understand what he was trying to say, or at least I believe I do. But he still shouldn't have said it. I gingerly wash my face, feeling my arm protest and strain when I move it around. I don't think I'll be getting much renovation work in today. At least my right hand is still functional. Maybe I could still paint? I look up at my reflection, at my pale skin and my even paler lips. I need to get something to eat, find Austin, and get past this silly fight. I think it's officially our first, but that's okay. All couples must have them at some point. Humans will be humans. The important part is not that we've fought but rather, how we overcome it, how quickly we make up.

Nausea grips my belly, drawing me down to my knees with a gasp when I make the mistake of reaching out and gripping the wall with my injured arm. I bend over the toilet, coughing and heaving, unable to get anything up but bile. *If I'm going to be sick, I may as well have something to vomit up. Not having anything is almost worse.* I don't hear the knock on my door because I'm too busy hunching over the toilet.

"Amy?" I expect it to be Christy, but it's not. This time, it's Tease. She comes up to the bathroom door and pauses outside of it, leaning against the frame and looking down at me. We haven't known each other for long, but I like her very much. I have fantasies that one day, I'll have a group of friends much like Austin does. My very own Beck, Gaine, and Kimmi. I hope Tease is one of them. And the fact that she's having a baby is even more exciting. I'll get to be a part of the child's life. "You're having worse morning sickness than me," she says with a small laugh. I think it's meant to be a joke.

"What?" I ask, my fingers clenching tight. I cry out and wrap my arm over my chest, touching the bandage gently as I turn to look at Tease.

"You should come see Didi again," she says, her red brows wrinkling in worry. "I think she's down in what used to be the kitchen." Tease smiles again, but I don't move from where I'm sitting. My heart is thumping a million miles a minute. *Oh dear.* I swallow hard and think very carefully. My life has been such a whirlwind lately, I've not been going about things as carefully as perhaps I should have. *When was the last time I took a birth control pill?* I think about it hard, but my mind is all muddled with fear. I've been taking them regularly. Well, mostly. Okay, maybe not mostly but often ... *Jesus, Amy.* And then, there are seven pills in each pack that don't have hormones. I certainly don't remember taking any week long breaks with Austin. My throat gets tight.

"Oh Lord, help me," I whisper as Tease bends down next to me. I look her straight in her green eyes and try not to pass out. "I think I might be pregnant." She blinks at me a couple of times and then opens her mouth, shuts it, opens it again.

"Why would you think that?" she says, and I

remember her telling me that she and Beck never used condoms nor was she on any birth control. *It was like we were asking for it*, she'd said with a smile. I'd tried to be good, but everything was so up in the air.

"I don't … " I pause and force myself to smile. It feels like my face is being stretched like taffy. "Maybe I'm overreacting?" I ask instead, forcing myself to my feet with a grunt. Tease helps me up and moves out of the bathroom, waiting with a bemused expression on her face. *Just because my boobs are sore, and I feel slightly dizzy, and I keep throwing up, that doesn't mean a darn thing.* I smooth my hands down the front of yesterday's jeans and wish fervently for a set of clean clothes.

"Is there a reason you might be pregnant?" Tease asks and then takes a deep breath. "I mean, do you use condoms regularly or … ?" She spreads her hands and then shrugs. Tease might only be eighteen, but she's a hell of a lot more worldly than I am. I feel for a moment as if I'm speaking to my big sister.

"We never use condoms; I was on the pill," I whisper, twisting my hands and glancing over at the mirror to my right. I stand up straight and put my hand on my belly. No change there – it's as flat as it's always been. "But I … didn't always take them. And we didn't stop … " I try to figure out how to phrase this without being vulgar. No, I did not sleep with Austin during any heavy days of my period, but I ... certainly didn't abstain for the entire seven day span either. Can one get pregnant during their period? I feel ridiculously misinformed at the moment. A product of my upbringing – I was no *Carrie*, but I didn't learn about my period until *after* I'd started it. At least Mama was with it enough to get me the pills in the first place. *Oh, the dichotomy of it all.* "Oh my."

Tease's eyebrows draw together and she shrugs again.

"I have some leftover ... sticks," she says with a slight smile, brushing some ruby red hair back from her face. Since she and Beck both have green eyes, red hair, and pale skin, I imagine their child coming out looking much the same. Unless, of course, I'm wrong and they end up with a brunette. "Come on. Let's go back to the hotel for awhile, and grab something to eat." I try to smile back at her, but I don't feel particularly well, gunshot wound aside. This is a different kind of sickness, a fear that's worming its way into my gut. *What ever would Austin say?*

CHAPTER 13
AMY

"It would be kind of fun, right?" Tease says, poking at the remains of her sandwich. She's sitting on the end of Austin's and my bed with her plate on her lap, dressed in a clean black tank top and fresh jeans. I've still got my robe on, a towel wrapped around my wet hair. Showering was not as pleasant as it should've been. I had to wrap my wounded arm with plastic, and then struggle to shampoo and condition my hair with only one hand. From shoulder to wrist, there's a dull, throbbing ache, numbed just barely by the ibuprofen and the Tylenol I took together. The ride over here was bad enough, all that jostling around, struggling to stay seated on Beck's bike. He made me sit in front of him while he drove me back, convinced that Austin would chop off his … well, he made a dirty reference to his *testicles* … if he let me ride my bike back injured. Not that there's any way to know that – Austin and his motorcycle are gone.

I didn't ask Beck if he knew where his friend had gone. To be honest, I don't want to know. He'll be back soon, I'm sure of it.

"What would be kind of fun?" I ask, throwing a wary sidelong glance at the box sitting next to the TV. *This is ridiculous*, I keep telling myself, even though I know it's not. Even if I hadn't messed up with the pills, they're not one hundred percent effective. This is something I should be doing regularly anyway. Especially since I didn't have my period last month. It took some hard thinking while I was in the shower, but as I scrolled back through the days, I could only remember the month before. *My word, Amy Cross. How have you become so scatterbrained?* If I'd been paying attention, instead of luxuriating in the arms of my real life book boyfriend, I might have noticed.

I move casually towards the pink box and pick it up, feeling the two pregnancy tests inside slide around.

"To have babies at the same time," she says, picking up her plate and setting it back on the room service tray that's balanced on the table near the balcony doors. Tease glances over her shoulder and throws me a winning smile. I'm not sure if she's serious or if she's simply trying to make me feel better. Either way, I appreciate it.

"I guess so," I say, wondering if this is something I should be excited about or if I should be dreading the results. *Do I want a baby?* I've never really given much thought to it. I was raised with a preconceived notion of how my life would go. *Grow up, get married, have kids, help out in the church.* That was it. So I never really had the opportunity to even consider *not* having children.

My stomach turns as I suck in a deep breath and brace myself. I suppose there's no reason going over this in my head until I know for sure anyway. I give Tease a look, and she passes me a thumbs-up right back.

"Okay then," I say, more to myself than to her. "Let's just get this over with, shall we?" I head into the bathroom and shut the door before I can change my mind. Ignorance is bliss and all that, right? I set the box on the counter, pull up and my robe and get ready to … *pee.* It doesn't sound quite so scary when you put it that way, right? Right?

I take both tests and set them on the counter, slumping to the tile floor while I wait. Above me, the fan whirs, blocking out any sound from outside the bathroom. I realize that the box says *results in one minute* with a very excited couple of exclamation points after it, but I sit there for a good fifteen minutes, pulling the towel off of my hair and brushing the brunette strands out with slow strokes.

I am a new woman. An independent woman. I am in a motorcycle club. I make my own decisions. I survived a gunshot wound. I repeat comforting phrases in my head, one sentence for each brush stroke, until my hair is fully combed and lying softly against the fluffy white fabric of the robe. I wrap it closer around myself and sit up on my knees, grabbing one of the white sticks and pulling it towards me.

There are two pink lines in the center oval. Two distinct lines that, according to the key on the side, mean only one thing. *Pregnant.* I swallow hard, my mouth suddenly dry and throw the stick into the garbage can near the toilet. I close my eyes and grab onto the second one, flopping against the wall and sending up a silent prayer. What exactly that prayer is about, I'm not sure. I'm still conflicted inside, still not sure how I feel about any of this. Maybe if Austin and I hadn't had a fight last night, I wouldn't be feeling this way. But then, it wasn't much of a squabble, and I'm certain, *certain*, that when he gets here, everything will be okay. He'll apologize, and we'll move on.

I open my eyes and look at the second test. *Pregnant.* Two lines stare up at me, and I can almost hear them speaking in quiet commentary. *How do you think she'll handle this? With grace, like a lady? Or petulantly, like a child?* I ignore the whirring in my head and stand up. Tease is going through this very same thing, although with a rather different attitude than me. She seems to be thrilled.

I throw the second test into the garbage can and rinse my hands before stepping out of the bathroom with a sigh.

"Tease, it ... " It's not Tease sitting in my room but Austin. I let out a small shriek before clamping my hands over my mouth.

"Whoa there, doll. Relax, it's only me." Austin stands up, quite the vision in his leather vest and boots, blonde hair sticking to his sweaty forehead. I do my best not to swoon and cross my arms over my chest. I refuse to let my gaze slide back to the bathroom, to the trash can and its contents. I'm not going to withhold this information from Austin, but I need a moment to process before I bring him into the fold. He tries to smile at me, the small scar on his lip tugging at his mouth. "Are you that unhappy to see me?"

"I'm not unhappy to see you," I say, taking a deep breath and letting it out slowly. The cumbersome robe suddenly feels like lingerie under his gaze, and I am all too aware of how easy it would be for him to pull it off my shoulders. "I just didn't expect to see you. Where's Tease?"

Austin takes a few steps towards me, pausing with his hands hovering over my arms. I know he's thinking about the gunshot, maybe about our argument last night.

"She excused herself when I got in." Austin grins, but I can tell it's not entirely genuine. "I think she was worried we might want to get it on." I pull back a bit and give him a look.

"We are most certainly *not* getting it on," I say, the words a bit stilted coming from my mouth. I glide back into the bathroom with him on my heels and pull some toilet paper from the roll, pretending to wipe my face before I drop it in the garbage can to cover up the evidence. "Not until we talk about what happened last night."

I put my hands on the bathroom counter and pretend I don't feel his hard body looming over me, hands quivering, pants getting tighter by the second. It's hardly even possible for the two of us to coexist in the same small space without falling to it like rutting beasts. The corner of my lip twitches. *Pregnant.* The word is a whisper, caught on the sound of the rotating fan and getting lodged in my ear.

"Amy, I was a shithead last night. I shouldn't have said what I said. O' course I'm glad I dragged your sweet, little ass out of that one-horse town. I saw some things that really fucked with my head yesterday, and I reacted. Badly. I'm just so fuckin' worried about you."

"I'm fine, Austin. I like it here."

"Yeah, but you got *shot*, Miss Cross. *Shot*. And this is not an isolated incident. We lost ten members of our group. What if you had been one of them?" I understand where Austin is coming from. What he needs to realize is that I don't care. I mean, I do care about the lives lost and the tragedy, but I don't care about the danger of it. If that's the price I have to pay to be with him, to live this life, then I'll take the risk.

"Austin," I begin, turning around and finding that my ass is pressed up tight against the counter. He's so close, I can feel his breath on my cheek when he leans in close and breathes in my scent. "I want to be with you."

"What if I'm not good enough, Amy?" he says, his voice dropping low. Austin's big, beautiful hands come up and brush gently against the sleeves on my robe. I think he's afraid to touch me. I put my hands on his chest and push him back a step. "I'm a shit President, and maybe I'm a shit … lover. Boyfriend. Whatever it is you want to call me. I ain't ever done anything like this before." He smiles slightly. "When it comes to relationships, I'm almost as virginal as you were."

I grab the sides of his stubbled face, enjoying the rough texture against my smooth flesh.

"You are *not* a shit President. Why can't you see in yourself what everybody else sees in you, Austin? You have a strong heart and a sound mind. That's all there is to it." I let go of him and step back, watching his dark eyes follow me with desperation and hunger. "Now, apologize for last night, and we'll move on." I try to make my voice sound chipper, but it comes out fractured and wanting. I just found out there's a very good chance I'm pregnant, and I'm already prepared to hop back in the sack? *For shame, Miss Cross. For shame.* I suppose it's too late to worry about such things.

"I really am sorry for what I said, Amy. You needed me, and I acted like a donkey's dick." I chuckle and slap a hand over my mouth as my heels bump into the garbage can with the pregnancy tests. I've moved back as far as I can go. My breath flutters in my throat like a sparrow, tiny wings beating against my insides, giving me that nervous stomachache again.

"You're forgiven," I say, watching him breathe a sigh of relief. Austin runs his fingers through his hair, the tattoos on his arms shining bright under the harsh fluorescent lighting from above. Austin must be quite handsome to be able to stand under these lights and not suffer for it. "But you're still not okay, are you?"

"I'm a little stressed, sugar. I won't lie to you." He turns and leans his back against the wall, examining me with restraint and desire both mixing in his dark gaze. "I don't want to fail, but it seems like that's all I'm doin' lately. Messin' up and tripping over my own damn feet." I reach my fingers down to the tie on my robe. I debate briefly on whether I should tell him about the tests or not, but decide against it. Not when he's feeling this stressed out. I don't want the moment to be anxious, and how can I expect him to react positively when I'm still not sure how I feel about the whole thing?

"It'll be okay," I tell him, untying the robe and sliding it down my shoulders. I wince a bit when it moves over my bandage, but I keep my facial expression pleasant. *Sex is to guys what a reading session in front of a fire is to chicks – chocolate and wine included.* I thank Sali Bend for her advice and let the robe hit the floor in a pool of white terry cloth around me. "Give it another chance and you'll see." The restraint in Austin's eyes breaks, and he strides across the room towards me, clutching my elbows with such gentle strength that it almost brings tears to my eyes.

I kiss him hard and deep, pressing the line of my naked body against his. Even if he hasn't said it, I know he loves me. No one could kiss like that if they didn't feel that breaking, soul shattering ache inside. I pull away suddenly and grab his wrist, dragging him into the bedroom but past the bed. Austin's blonde brows climb towards his hairline as I pause in front of the sliding door to the balcony and slide it open.

Hot summer heat creeps in, clashing with the cool air from the air conditioner. I smile at his puzzled look and glance out at the nearby balconies. There's nobody else around and even if there were, they can – excuse my French – go *fuck* themselves. That final scene in my Sali and Glance novel is haunting me, and while I'm feeling like this, this braveness to the point of fault, I might as well go for it.

"Sit down," I whisper to Austin, grabbing his shirt in my fingers and pulling it up and over his head. He lets me, watching as I toss it to the cement patio beneath my bare feet. The pavement is hot, but not unbearably so, like a match for the fire that's burning inside.

"And this is why I like you, Amy Allison Cross. You never fail to surprise me." Austin sits down on the lounge chair, swinging his feet up and reaching down to unbutton his pants. I wait there, standing unabashedly

naked in the warm air. I liken my mood to the gunshot
– this might hurt later but I might as well be in mental
shock now. *Screw it.*

I let my eyes rake across the pistol tattoos on his
collarbone, the demon wing on his shoulder, the skulls,
the roses. As if having the body of a Greek god wasn't
enough, my man is decorated, too. A small flush creeps
into my face. *My man. Mine.* I feel a slight
possessiveness wash over me and hug myself tight,
taking a deep breath as Austin frees himself from his
pants.

"At least you have the good sense to listen to me," I
say with a small smile, swinging my leg over the chair so
that I'm straddling him but not sitting down, not yet. I
let my head fall back as his hands slide up the backs of
my thighs, cutting a path of pleasure through my
sensitive flesh. He caresses my ass next, lingering there
as he kneads the soft flesh between his fingers before
moving up and taking a firm hold of my hips.

Austin leans forward and presses his mouth against
my belly, kissing me with a hungry heat that threatens
to overwhelm and consume me. But that's okay. I want
to be *devoured.* When he goes for my breasts, I stop
him by bending down, sitting against him and stroking
his cock along my pussy, but I don't let him enter me.
Not yet. My hands come around his neck, enjoying the

feel of his hair as we kiss again, rubbing our bare chests together. The breeze picks up and flutters my own hair around my face, mixing my brunette with his blonde. I run my fingers across the strong muscles in Austin's neck and shoulders, sliding them up his throat and enjoying the strong, sturdy feeling in his jaw, his cheekbones, his straight nose.

I close my eyes and pretend like I'm blind, like the only way I'll be able to tell what he looks like is if I feel. I smooth my thumbs over Austin's brows, sliding my lips against his but not kissing, just tasting, breathing.

I decide to keep my bravery going.

"I love you, Austin Sparks," I whisper, keeping my eyes squeezed shut, so I can't see the expression on his face. I kiss him hard and fast, reaching down and guiding him inside of me. I don't want to force the words out of him, just simply let him know how I feel. I've already said it, so there's no taking it back anyway. Not that I'd want to. Love isn't something that should feel shameful, not when it's this beautiful.

Austin's cock slides deep, penetrating me straight to the core while the sound of traffic whizzes by on the highway. It's exhilarating, thinking that someone could walk out onto their balcony and see us. It's not likely, but the thought is what makes this exciting.

I press my cheek tight to Austin's and move my

body, grinding myself into him. I move at an agonizingly slow pace, moaning when his hands find my hips and rest there, quivering with violent need. But he holds back, turning my insides to jelly when I think of all the hard strength that's in his muscles, all the power. He could so easily take control, but he doesn't, letting me keep the rhythm. His fingers stay hovering above my flesh, touching but not squeezing, resting, caressing, feeling me. After a few moments, he guides them downwards and finds my clit.

I sit back a bit, splaying my hands out flat against his muscular chest. The heat of the day is already drawing sweat from his skin, slicking his body with a wetness that very nearly drives me insane. I enjoy the smooth planes of his pecs, feeling them up the same way I felt his face. When my hands start to dip low on Austin's belly, I force my eyes to open up, catching his gaze open and wild, fierce. *He really is like an alpha wolf, isn't he?* I think as I slide both hands down, ignoring the twinge in my upper arm. I cup my hands around his as he rubs my clit, bringing me to orgasm in a burst of sound that escapes from my mouth, flying up into the sky like a bird.

CHAPTER 14
Austin

The next morning, before the sun even comes up, I'm layin' in bed holdin' Amy when my phone rings. Jesus himself only knows how shitty things must be if someone's calling before sunrise. Without waking up my woman, I roll over and grab my cell, heading out onto the balcony, confident that nobody else is up at this Godawful hour. Hope not, or they're going to get a face full o' my junk.

I don't recognize the number, so I answer it with a gruff, "Austin Sparks."

"It's Tax." The President of Seventy-seven Brothers doesn't wait for me to ask questions. "I've got some information that I thought you might find useful." There's a sound of rustling cloth and a grunt. "I'm calling you as a professional courtesy." He pauses. "And because you have my little sister in your care."

"Shit, I ain't gonna like this, am I?" I ask, glancing over my shoulder. Amy is stirring with a murmur, her face angelic in the almost darkness of an early morning. I look back out towards the city. The greater metro area here is known as Bandit, Tennessee. Our new turf. Someday soon, I'm going to have to start making calls to the nearest MCs. At least for right now, this entire area is wholly unoccupied.

"I got some more information about the guns, among other things." Tax sighs, his voice heavy. It doesn't sound like he's had much sleep the past two nights. "You were right – M16s. Automatic. Illegal as a bare naked jog through Central Park, twice as deadly. You might want to watch your back. Bested by Crows and Broken Dallas are merging together, and they are pissed. Your previous President, Kent Diamond, made some deals to traffic guns, drugs, women, you name it. When you killed him and the Walker brothers, a lot of the information died with them. But not their promises. They made deals with some rather unsavory fuckin' folks. Now they're on the hook for not keeping up with their contracts." Tax sighs as my hand grips the railing of the balcony with rigid fingers. "Meaning *you're* on the hook for the deals that fell through. Just thought I'd let you know. Keep your guard up and don't you dare let a fucking thing happen to my sister, or you'll be praying for Bested by Crows to take you."

"How do you know all this shit?" I ask, listening as a moan breaks through the phone. Not a pleasant sound, more like torturous. *Shit.* Tax sighs.

"Doesn't matter. Use the information I just gave you, finish your clubhouse, and keep my sister and her baby safe." Tax hangs up the phone before I can respond, leaving me with a rapidly beating heart and the monster of panic eating up my insides. Nobody ever said this job was easy, but this, I didn't expect.

I stand on the balcony for awhile, trying to take control of myself and my emotions. *I am not a weak man*, I tell myself. *But it feels like the burden of proof is hanging heavy on my shoulders. I need to prove myself with actions, not words.*

I gather myself together and move back into the hotel room, finding Amy awake, sitting up in bed with her arms wrapped around her knees. She looks contemplative. I set my phone on the table near the balcony door and close it behind me.

"You're up early," she says, a question in her voice. I need to tell her what I know. Fuck, I need to tell *everyone* in Triple M what I know, and then I need to make sure we're prepared. I just have to figure out the best way to do that. "Everything okay?"

"For the moment, sugar," I say, not surprised to see that my cock is more than happy to find her awake. Rain or shine, Mr. Sparks never lets me down. I move towards her, climbing onto the bed and sliding my arm around Amy's waist. I press a kiss to her throat and taste her pulse. "How's your arm?" Amy clears her throat sharply, and a spike of anticipation cuts through my stomach. *Goddamn it, what now?* I wonder as I sit back and take stock of her expression.

Determined. Fearful. Prideful. Happy. Sad. Like looking through a damn kaleidoscope.

Amy brushes some of her beautiful chestnut hair behind an ear.

"Austin," she begins, and her voice is dead serious. I pull the blankets over my erection and wait there for her to finish speaking. No sense in trying to rush this. I almost don't even want to know. I wonder if this has something to do with those three little words, those cursed, Godforsaken syllables that have been plaguing me for awhile now. *I love you.* I do love Amy, but I don't want to say anything until I'm ready. I could say it back, sure. Wouldn't kill me, but it wouldn't mean what she wants it to mean. I'm not sure what I'm waiting for exactly or if I'm even waiting for anything, but the time isn't right yet. I'm sure I'll feel it when it is.

Amy turns to me, putting her hands on top of mine. I can't keep my gaze away from her arm, from the bandage that shouldn't even be there. If I'd protected her proper, it wouldn't have happened. *And you still haven't figured out who did it. Get your crap together, Austin.*

"Excuse me, sorry," Amy says, letting her lashes flutter closed and her forehead drop low. She leans forward and presses her face against my bicep. This overwhelming protective urge tears into me, and I find myself folding Amy into my arms and looking up at the ceiling with a prayer fluttering on my lips. *Don't let me fuck this shit up.* "This is a difficult subject to broach … "

"You don't gotta tell me if you don't want to," I whisper, dropping my chin to her hair. I wonder if I can get away without MC bullshit clogging up my damn veins today, just spend a day figuring shit out. I'd be nice to do somethin' normal with Amy for once, take her out to dinner, go for a walk, whatever. "We can just … I dunno, tear out that ugly ass vanity in the downstairs bathroom." Amy chuckles and lifts her face up, smiling brightly at me. I brush some hair away from her forehead.

"Thanks for making this easier," she says, and I raise an eyebrow.

"You're welcome?" I say, pulling her into my lap, breathing hot breath against her throat. Amy squirms, rubbing her body along my cock. I'm about to push inside of her when she says it.

"Austin, I'm pregnant."

CHAPTER 15

Austin pauses, grabbing onto my arms and causing me to bite my lip in pain when his hand brushes my bandage.

"Shit, sugar," he breathes, letting go. "I'm sorry." I sit back, sliding a safe distance away from his genital region. There is no way on earth I'm going to be able to think clearly if we're pressed together like that. I grab the white sheets and tuck them around myself, moving away so that the only parts of us that are touching are covered with fabric. I don't look away though. I keep my eyes completely focused on Austin's. "What ... what did you ... " He looks disoriented, like he's gotten lost somewhere inside of himself.

"I mean, I suppose I could be wrong, but I took two

tests today and they were both positive." I keep watching Austin's face for some sign of how I should feel. Right now, I'm not exactly enjoying what I see. "And when I finally sat down and thought about it, I realized I hadn't had my period last month." Austin stays silent, sitting there with his back against the headboard. I wait a whole minute for him to respond, but he doesn't. He sits there, staring at me. "Austin?"

"Amy," he says back, voice soft but not angry, not disappointed, just empty. He's mulling over the idea just like I am. Austin runs his fingers through his hair while I wait, trying to be patient but unable to stop the thoughts that are racing through my head. Tease said Beck whooped for joy when she told him, took her in his arms and made love to her. This, this isn't like that at all.

"You don't have to say anything," I tell him, starting to stand up. "I just thought you should know." I let the sheets slip aside and start to walk away when Austin grabs me around the right wrist and tugs me back towards him, enfolding me in his arms and pressing his face into my back. The stubble on his jaw tickles me, and I squirm.

"God woman," he says, voice rough and bursting with emotion. "How long have you known?"

"Only since yesterday afternoon," I admit as I let

Austin pull me back to the bed and lay me out flat on my back. He leans over me, brushing his fingers down my cheek. "Why does it matter?"

"I'm just glad you told me," he says, and I have a real hard time reading the emotion in his face. I don't get much time to examine it because Austin draws back and flips me over, pulling my ass to the edge of the bed and pressing his dick between my cheeks. *Oh goodness.* I dig my fingers into the bedspread, and try to figure out what exactly is going on here. Is this a joyous ... er, union? Or is Austin trying to fuck me for lack of a better alternative? I can't tell.

"Austin, what are you doing?" I ask, breath a rare commodity in my lungs. *I can hardly breathe.* He chuckles behind me and the sound makes the hair on the back of my neck stand on end. I lean into him, and bite my lip as he glides against me, teasing but not entering. *You wickedly cruel, cruel man. How can I be doing this when I have no idea what it is you're thinking?*

"Celebratin'," Austin whispers harshly as he slams into me, filling me up with a sharp burst of sound from his throat. I press my face into the bed, smelling laundry detergent overlaid with the sharp scent of sex. We had quite a good time in here last night – it didn't end on the balcony. Last night's sex was so vastly

117

different than this, almost fuzzy around the edges, soft. There's nothing soft about what Austin's doing to me right now.

"You want to have a baby with me?" I ask. Well, I suppose *ask* isn't the right word. More accurately, I moan the phrase, letting it fall from my lips and hang in the air around us. The phrase feels so foreign, wrapping around and tangling our souls together tight. I hope this is really what Austin wants. It's hard for me to tell.

"I want you," Austin growls, holding onto me tight, pounding so quick and hard and fast I can almost imagine that we're strangers meeting in an alley for an illicit tryst. Not by any stretch of the imagination would I call this making love. "You're mine, Amy. I told you that."

"And you're mine," I say, trying to keep my voice firm, even with *la petite mort* sneaking her dirty little fingers into the mess. Austin grips me tight, sliding one hand up to tangle in my hair, pulling my face up and forcing me to arch my back into him. Perhaps I should feel slighted we're not having a deep, verbose conversation about this, discussing options or plans or logicality. But I'm not. That's not Austin. Austin speaks with actions and intents instead of words. I feel this protective possessiveness radiating from him, this uncouth display of affection. He is, after all, a dirty biker boy.

"You're *my* baby and if you're gonna be pregnant with anybody's seed, it's gotta be mine." I moan, feeling the sound gurgle up from my throat, enjoying a guilty slice of primal bliss as I clench around him, my body working hard to achieve what it's already conquered, milking his seed from his cock with tight, fluttering pulses of muscle. I come first, resting in the hands of *the little death*, feeling her wrap her dark cloak around me and drag me under.

CHAPTER 16
Austin

"Shit, shoot, and crap in a barrel," Beck chortles, slapping his thigh and raising his beer bottle up for a toast. "Me and you, we're like two peas in a damn pod."

"You're a crazy son of a bitch," I tell him, but I manage to clink the brown glass of my bottle against his. Gaine joins us with a slight frown, and Kimmi follows after. As we settle back on our stools and pretend the whole damn restaurant isn't staring straight at these four fools at the bar, Beck starts his blabbering again.

"Wandering through life, a couple of ol' bachelors," he begins, and I groan. He doesn't like when I listen to Nickelback on the intercom, and I don't like when he starts off on his stories. "Find ourselves a couple of much younger ladies."

"Jesus Christ," Gaine says, leaning his elbow on the counter. Kimmi just sits there smilin' away.

"And within a span shorter than a pony's stride, we buy some houses, and knock our sweethearts up. Living the American dream, amen!"

"You been down here drinking before I even called your ass up, weren't you?" Beck wrinkles his red brows at me, green eyes sparkling. He's genuinely thrilled with all of this, and it's not just his usual sense of good humor. Beck is *happy*.

"Shoot, no," he says which is about ninety-nine percent likely to be a lie. "Me and Tease were pickin' out baby names, like a proper couple." Kimmi wraps her nails around his bicep and snuggles against his arm.

"I'm going to be an auntie times *two*," she squeals, fluttering her long, fake lashes against her cheeks. I watch as she takes another swig of beer. "Amy's probably even further along than Tease, huh?"

"Always trying to outdo me, ain't ya, Austin Sparks," Beck says, narrowing his eyes and pointing his beer bottle in my direction. "I see right through you."

"He's definitely drunk," Gaine interjects, ordering up some whiskey and setting his beer aside. He folds his hands behind his head, sitting up straight and staring at Beck and me both with a measuring gaze. His dark hair is all scruffy and out of place and there's definitely a hickey or two peeking out the top of his shirt, but I don't say a damn thing about it. None of my business anyway.

"Shit, you're just jealous because you know Mireya Sawyer is incapable of makin' babies. Demons can't breed."

"Fuck you *and* your dead grandma, Beck," Mireya counters, appearing behind him and reaching around to steal his beer. She looks me straight in the face and my stomach clenches tight. I don't feel anything romantic for her, but she's still my friend and I love her. It's just our sordid history that's got a knot of fear curling around my insides. "What are you guys celebrating? Tease's pregnancy?"

"Yes and no," Kimmi says, sitting up straight and tinkering with her dangly earrings. She slides her green eyes over to Mireya's brown ones. "Amy's pregnant, too."

"Amy?!" Mireya practically chokes on the word, giving me a look that's hard to decipher. "Jesus Christ, you guys. It takes a village to raise a child and now we've got two?"

"We'll return the favor when Gaine finally figures out how to sow his wild oats in your devil womb." Beck chuckles at his own joke and starts in on a new bottle.

"You are such a fucking dick," Mireya says, scowling at my friend and coming around to stand next to Gaine. I turn to look at her, not because I want to, but because I can feel her eyes burning lasers into me. It's safer at this point *not* to look away. If I do, she might just incinerate me. "When did you find out about this?"

"About," I glance at my watch, "twelve hours ago." I look back up at Mireya, standing with her hands on her hips, her jacket hanging loosely off her shoulders and flashing me perfectly bronzed skin and a fancy red top that I'm sure is all for Gaine's benefit. "Why?"

"I guess that would explain your mood today," Gaine says, dropping his arm around Mireya's waist and holding her close. I am such a dense motherfucker. I spent *years* watching these two prance around each other, and I never once noticed anything between them. I'm going to have to try real hard not to make the same mistakes with Amy. I don't want to be oblivious and stupid anymore. I spin my bottle between my hands and wonder what she's really doing upstairs in that bathtub. She says she's planning on reading, but who knows? I just hope she's not upset. I tried real hard to be attentive today, to talk to her, kiss her, hold her. We haven't exactly discussed the issue at hand, but I'm sure we'll get to it. It took me a second to process what she was saying, but after I got over the initial shock, I felt okay. It's a lot of responsibility, but I have to man my ass up. If I'm going to be a dad, I'm going to be a damn good one, and I sure as hell ain't going to let my kid be as much of a fuck up as me.

A baby.

Shit. Who woulda thought?

I take another drink of beer.

"This really puts the pressure on me to take care of shit," I say, thinking of Tax's phone call this morning.

"I know," Gaine responds, setting his lips in a thin line. "But it's going to be okay. We'll get through this crap like we always do. Ghosts can be banished. We'll get rid of Kent's leftover garbage eventually and live happily ever after." He smiles at me, and I almost want to believe his fairytale dreams. Must be nice bein' Gaine.

"You're having a baby with your sweetheart. Perk up." Beck slaps me on the back, guzzling beer and clinking his glass against Kimmi's. I smile at him, raising my own bottle for yet another toast. I guess the question at this point isn't *what if I'm not good enough.* I'm going to *have* to be good enough. There is no choice in the matter, not if I love Amy Cross, and I do. I look down at the polished stone counter beneath my hands and take hold of that possessive urge I feel inside. Amy is *mine*, and this baby is *mine.* Fuck, if you want to get technical, that fucking *house* is mine. This club is mine.

I look up at the bartender, seeing him but not really looking at him. My gaze goes straight through to somewhere else. I take one last sip of my drink and set it down on the counter. What the hell am I doing down here when my lady is upstairs?

"Excuse me, boys," I tell them, rolling my shoulders and trying to work out a hard day's worth of kinks. "Ladies." I nod at Mireya and Kimmi, ignoring the catcalling that follows me across the burgundy carpeting of the restaurant and into the elevator doors. I lean against the wall and shake my head. "Fuckin' A, Austin. Why on earth would God give your stupid ass a baby?" I answer my own question. "Maybe to wake me up inside and get my blood going? Maybe that's it?" So I walk out of that elevator with a smile on my face, and a heart ready to cast aside doubt. Everything seems like it's going to be peachy Goddamn keen until I find two of my guys slumped on the floor at the end of the hallway. I check their pulses, but they're not dead, just knocked out. "What the fuck?" I've got my cellphone out and I'm dialing up Beck's number before I even make it to the door of my hotel room. "Get your asses up here. Now." I don't wait to listen to what he has to say, sliding my key in and shoving my way into the room with sweat beading on my lip and soaking into my T-shirt. "Amy?"

I move through the bedroom and into the bathroom, finding the bathtub full of water, full of bubbles, with a book lying closed on the countertop. Amy is not fucking in here. I spin around, in full panic mode now, eyes searching desperately for a sign, any Goddamn sign that she's okay. I move back into the room and find her cellphone on the dresser next to the TV. Amy's duffel bag is wide open, clothes strewn across the floor haphazardly. That's not like her at all. Either she left in a hurry or someone made her leave in a hurry.

"Fuck." My voice is quivering with abject fear, and the muscles in my hands are so tight that my fingers curl painfully into my palm. After all this, this doubt, this stupidity on my part, I finally decide to push past it when I'm proven right. I am a shitty motherfucking leader.

CHAPTER 17
Amy

I don't want to say that Margot is being particularly cruel to me, but I also can't say that I appreciate being kidnapped either. Most especially when I had a bubble bath and a book waiting for me.

"I didn't want to do this," Margot says, voice hard but only on the outside. Deep down, I can sense this painful bite of vulnerability. It gives me some hope where hope is much needed. Right now, I'm handcuffed, bound and blindfolded in the back of a car – apparently not all motorcycle clubs do their dirty work with bikes. "And I didn't mean to shoot you either. I might've let my anger get the better of me." I feel the car pause, the engine rumbling as we idle to a stop. A minute or so later, we're moving again, my body slamming into the seats as Margot takes off with a jolt. I grunt when my injured arm gets crushed behind me, the insides of my eyelids flashing white with pain. "I thought you were Kimmi." The anger in Margot's voice boils behind her words as we take a sharp turn. "But there was no way I was getting in there to kidnap her. Let's be honest, Amy. You were the easy choice." I smell the scent of cigarette smoke drifting lazily into my nostrils. "Tease would've been a better bargaining chip for me, but oh well." Margot sighs and keeps driving.

I try my best to keep a good humor, but I know the sorts of things that could happen to me. If Margot's working alone, maybe she'll simply use me as a hostage, but if she really is still in with Bested by Crows and Broken Dallas, I could be seeing the ugly side of this life with my own two eyes.

But no. No. Austin will come through for me. I know he will. I take a deep breath and try to put the trust in him that he doesn't yet have in himself.

I don't get to ask any questions. This is not a Sali Bend novel. *Where the fuck are you taking me*? *Are you nuts*? *I'm carrying a baby here. This is going to be hard enough, thank you.* If it were a Sali book, I'm certain I would've escaped by now, used a knife that I was hiding in my hair to somehow cut the bindings at my wrists. As things stand, I'm struggling just to keep the weight off my injured arm. Margot caught me by complete surprise, coming into the bathroom and catching me, quite literally, with my pants down. She forced me to dress quickly at gunpoint so unfortunately, I don't have anything fancy or clever up my sleeve.

Margot stops talking, leaving me to stew in silence, ears straining for the sound of motorcycles in the distance. *And I was having such a nice day, too,* I think, picturing the beautiful soft lavender color we'd painted in Kimmi's room. Well, Christy painted it mostly, and I helped with the edging, but Austin was there, too, working on the crown molding. I was hoping that when he came back upstairs, that we'd be able to talk. It wasn't in the cards, I suppose.

A biker gang, a biker boy, and a baby. It's an interesting combination, but I don't see why it couldn't work. In fact, when I close my eyes and let my mind go, I imagine it turning into something beautiful. Austin hasn't said anything outright, but I got a good feeling from him today, a positive aura. Sometimes, the thing you don't think you want is the only thing you really need.

I take deep breaths in through my nose and try to stay calm. Freaking out won't help anybody here. I assume Austin will rescue me, but I have to prepare for

the off chance that he doesn't come in time. I lay back
and try to come up with a plan.

CHAPTER 18
Austin

I have to push my mental problems aside. I ain't got time for that shit.

"Beck and me will head out now. Gaine, you rally the guys and get a group together. Send everyone else to the clubhouse to keep an eye on it." I slip Amy's cell into my back pocket and check to make sure my gun's in its holster. Everyone's lookin' at me like this a lost cause, and I don't like it. "Goddamn it! I didn't say straighten up your pantyhose and adjust your junk, I said *now*." I push past my friends and head down the stairs. I don't have the patience to wait in the elevator right now. I'm more than aware of what's at stake here. Amy's sanity, her dignity, her *life*. The life of my baby. "Fuck."

"Austin, slow down. You break your leg and you won't be of any use to Little Miss Cross." I ignore Beck, listening to the heavy fall of his footsteps as we careen down the stairs, moving out the heavy back door and across the hot heat of the parking lot. I try not to look at Amy's bike as I straddle mine. *We'll get her back. It'll be okay.* I have to keep telling myself that, even if I don't believe it. "Austin!" Beck grabs onto the front of my bike and leans in close. "We can't just run aimlessly around the city. We gotta get an idea of where we're going. If we take off in one direction, and Amy's on the other side of town, what good does that do us?" I close my eyes and take a deep breath. I know Beck's right. I get that, but that sick feeling in my gut, the one that made me so unsure of Amy and the clubhouse and this whole new life, it's changed. At least I can see what an idiot I've been.

"Okay, okay." I run my hands down my face and then drop them into my lap. I look up at the firm set of Beck's mouth. His determination makes me feel better, pulls me back from the edge for a moment. "So, when I left, Amy was alright. She obviously had enough time to run a bath. How long were we downstairs? A half an hour?" Beck nods as I bite at my lip and try to think real hard about this. The decisions I make now could affect whether Amy lives or dies. *If they rape her.* Oh

God. My precious little sugar. Adrenaline courses through me, and I feel my vision flicker with red. If I get my hands on these sons o' bitches, they're going to pray for death. "We didn't see anyone suspicious and none of the guys noticed anything, so I'm guessing there weren't many of 'em." I bite at my nail until it bleeds. "Let's say they got to her about fifteen minutes after I left. That gives Amy time to fix the bath and whatnot." I look up at the sky, at the muted orange tones in the distance and take a deep breath. "There's only one major highway heading out of here, and if you want to make good time, that's the way you'd go. Not on some backwater shit ass back roads, especially not when you're from out of town. My guess is they're going South. Nobody in their right minds would head North *towards* Seventy-seven Brothers' territory. So if we book it and make good time, maybe we can catch up to them before they disappear off the highway?"

Beck nods briskly, saluting me with a watery half-smile, and then jumps on the back of his bike. I lead us out of the parking lot, just seconds before Gaine and Mireya emerge from the hotel.

I tear out onto the street and disappear into the rush of traffic.

CHAPTER 19
Austin

Beck and I take the highway, keeping our eyes out for motorcycles.

"You think she'd be in a car or truck or somethin'?" I ask Beck. It's not exactly easy to wrestle a struggling lady onto your bike. Beck should know, considering he's done some recent kidnapping of his own. I doubt that whoever's got Amy will be as gentlemanly in their capture as my best friend though.

"Maybe," he replies through the intercom. I like the coiled snake of violence I hear hissing from his throat. It's good to have a crazy son of a bitch like Beck on your side. "But how the hell are we gonna know that?" I shake my head, even though I know he can't see me. He's right. If Amy's in one of these minivans, in the back of that sedan, in the center row of that SUV, how am I going to know that?

I grit my teeth and keep riding, uncertain if I'm even going in the right direction. I close my mind off and press forward. I can't sit and wait and do nothing, so I have to take a chance here, even if it's the wrong choice to make.

I weave in between the cars, searching windows for Amy's face, or maybe even somebody I might recognize from the fight. It feels like I'm searching for a needle in a haystack here, but I have to try. No matter what, I *have* to keep fighting. Guess that whole, *you never know how precious something is until you lose it* phrase is true. I'm missing Amy so fierce my chest feels like it's about to explode. I was nice today, but I wasn't nice *enough*. When Amy told me she was pregnant, I should've pulled her to me and told her I was happy, that there ain't a single other woman on this earth that I'd want to have a baby with. I should've told her *I love you*.

"Beck, I'm an idiot."

"I know you are, brother, and that's okay. A good woman can cure any ailment." I sigh into the mic.

"And I'm a shitty motherfucking leader."

"You're an inexperienced one. There's a big difference there, Sparks. Do you think I'd be putting

135

my life on the line for you if I didn't think you could do this? Fuck, I'd kick your ass off the throne and put Kimmi there if I didn't believe you capable."

"You're a good friend, Beck," I say, almost grudgingly.

"And you're a Goddamn brownnoser. Let's find Amy and be done with this, alright?"

"Amen," I whisper, jerking my bike to the right, sliding across traffic like a ghost. That's one of the nice things about riding a motorcycle – you become oblivious to the rest of the driving world. I speed ahead of Beck, crouching low, struggling to hold back the rush of adrenaline that's coursing through my veins. At this moment, I have no outlet for it. I've got to keep it bottled in until it's time to let loose.

I swing around a semi, and end up a few cars ahead of Beck, traveling along at speeds that are most definitely not going to fall within any legal limit. The road stretches out before me, numbing me to the situation and wrapping my soul up in the moment. Wind teases my shoulders, cutting through my leather jacket with knives that wake me up and make my memory so sharp it could cut. I see Amy bending over that Road King bike back in the day, so innocent but desperate to get out. I see myself, getting wrapped up in her mind, sweeping in and taking over. I've been thinking only of me, but it's really Amy whose life has changed the most.

I squeeze my hands so tight that they hurt, rocketing forward, eyes scanning the cars around me. I could get lucky here, catch a glimpse of Amy and act a hero savin' her from a fate worse than death. Instead, I get a phone call. I pull over to the side of the road, skidding into the gravel with a curse and a call to Beck over the intercom. My helmet comes off and I answer the phone without looking at the number.

"Austin Sparks." It's a voice I recognize. Goddamn it. Margot Tempe. Our rat is back and apparently quite eager to piss me the fuck off. "I know you're following me, but it has to stop. I'm not going to hurt Amy, but I need you to listen to me." My first urge is to tell her to piss the hell off, but that's not going to help my woman, and that's all that matters to me. *At least we're on the right track.* If she knows I'm following her, then we must've either passed her or shown up in her rearview mirror, right?

"What do you want, Margot?" I ask, wishing I had taken Beck's advice and shot the woman in the back of the damn head. But that wasn't the right decision to make, and I still stand before my original choice. I listen to the pause on the line, and I just know she didn't come up with this plan all on her own. "Why

Amy?"

"It's not really about Amy, Austin," she tells me as I scrub my fingers through my hair in a frustrated gesture. Beck slides in next to me and lifts his visor. I wave him away, gesturing at the highway with my left hand. Luckily, we've been friends long enough that he understands what I'm trying to say. Beck nods, puts his helmet back in place and takes off, merging into the traffic like a dancer or some shit. "This is about us."

"Who the fuck is *us*?" I ask, resisting the urge to make quotation marks with my fingers. Ain't nobody around to see that crap. I turn my head away from the traffic, wishing away the noise. I don't want to miss a damn word of this phone call. Doing that could change everything.

"*The Branded Kestrels*," Margot says, her voice muffled by the roar of a nearby semi. "The merger of Bested by Crows and Broken Dallas."

"You ain't nothin' to them, Margot," I say, trying to slice through her Achilles' heel with words. She's always been a weak girl. If joining these assholes is any indication, she still is. "You're less than the chrome in their rides, baby. If you're trying to buy a life with Amy's freedom, you're going to be sorely mistaken when it comes time for payment."

"I'm not buying anything," Margot snaps at me, and

I wonder how much her dignity's been taxed these last few months. I'm not bluffing here. She's probably a passing consequence to these guys, a toy to be used and discarded. It's a sad, sad fact in this world. I don't know why any woman would put themselves through that crap. "How would you have reacted to a dozen guys in cuts storming into the hotel? I dye my hair blonde and put on some fancy makeup, and Triple M hardly even notices me. Not a single fucking person recognized me until I got upstairs. How fucking pathetic are you?"

"Goddamn it, you stupid little bitch. What the fuck do you want? It ain't to chat my ear off, so let's hear it."

"Austin, we've got some contracts that have come due, and it's your fault we haven't been able to deliver. You're going to fulfill your end of the bargain whether you want to or not. The same offer still stands. Your women, their cuts, and money. I hope your last bank hit was kind to you because you're going to need as much as you can get. This isn't going away, Sparks. We have creditors and there are debts due. Somebody has to pay up, and it isn't going to be us."

"How the fuck is that going to get me Amy back?" I scream at her, beyond motherfucking frustrated. I've lost sight of Beck, but that's alright. As long as he's on her trail, or at the very least making the bitch nervous, that's exactly where he needs to be. I'll catch up. Then I'll pop Margot's petite little head from her shoulders.

"You have to make a choice, Austin Sparks. Your woman or your club." My heart starts to pound, so fast and hard it's like a hammer smashing a nail into my chest. I feel sick. "If you decide to choose your club, we'll keep Amy, and she'll be the first bitch in our stable of whores."

The phone clicks off, and I let out a scream.

CHAPTER 20
Austin

I dial Margot Tempe right back, seething with rage. It's back to this fuckin' shit again, is it? I won't just be rippin' heads from shoulders, I'm going to turn into a bona fide Beck clone, relishing the taste of blood and laughing when my hammer finds a soft skull to smash into.

"Excellent," she says, her small voice strong on the outside but crumbly and weak on the inside. She ain't a very impressive villain. "You have an answer already?"

"Margot Tempe, you slimy, backwater bogart piece o' shit from a horse's hoof, I swear on my mother's tits –
"

"Careful, Austin," she snaps, her voice full of hurt, like a petulant little brat in need of a spanking. "You're not in control this time, not really. You have one choice to make. Either you have an answer for me or you don't." I open my mouth to curse her grandma and their entire family, when Margot curses abruptly. "Fuck!"

The expletive coincides with a black sedan swerving in the lane closest to me. A silver SUV crashes into the side and the car spins like a top, cutting into the barbed wire fencing just twenty feet from where I'm sitting.

"Margot?" My voice is practically a whisper, drowning in the sound of her screams. The black sedan hits the ditch on the side of the road and flips straight over, sliding through the grass a couple dozen feet before coming to a steaming stop. "Margot?" I hear whimpering and the distant shouts of passersby. They echo doubly in my ear confirming my worst Goddamn nightmare. *This* is the fucking car. "Amy!"

I'm off my bike and running, hopping the fence and sprinting through the dry grass as fast as my leg will carry me. The sound of sirens blares in the distant, a background requiem for my pulsing fear.

"I didn't see them there!" the person in the silver SUV is screaming, slumped against the back of their vehicle, but they don't come any closer. "It was an accident." I leave the girl there to cry and slide to my knees next to the sedan. People are pulling over and rushing my way, but I ignore them, checking in the broken front window to find Margot alive, but bleeding. I ignore her, switching my attention to the back. I reach to open the door, but it's locked.

"Motherfucker," I growl, the adrenaline I was holding back springing free and overwhelming me. I don't even have time for logical thoughts, just base impulses to guide my hands. *Amy. Shit. Amy. Amy. Fuck.* I crawl back to the front, reaching my hand up and in, searching for the lock button. It only takes me a second, but I swear to Christ, it feels like a Goddamn century.

"My wife's in the back," I tell the first person to pause by my side. Amy might not actually be my wife, but she probably should be. "You help the girl in the front." I grab the handle and start to tug it open. The windows are tinted, so I have no idea what I'm getting myself into here. She could be dead. Maimed. The crumpled door resists my pull, catching on the ground and forcing me to use every ounce of strength I have to get it open. I manage to move it about halfway before it refuses to give another inch. Dropping back to my knees, I look inside and find Amy lying bloody and quiet on the roof of the car. She's bound and gagged, blindfolded. For the first time in a long, long while, tears come to my eyes, but I blink them away, pursing my lips with determination and crawling partially into the car to get a better look at her. "Amy?" I whisper, but she doesn't respond, doesn't even move. I can't tell if she's breathing or not. I reach down and slide the blindfold carefully away. I pretend that her body's made of glass, afraid to move her until the paramedics get here. I don't want anything I do right now to compromise her making it out of here alive.

Amy's eyes are shuttered tight, closed to the world, her dark lashes resting on her pale cheeks. There's blood dribbling down the side of her face, but no visible wound, at least not from this angle. I pull a knife out from my boot and use it to cut the gag away, pushing the rest of the world aside so I can focus on this. The fabric comes away in a wet clump, soaked through with blood and saliva. As soon as I peel it away however, Amy starts to groan, coughing and groaning as she rolls to the side and splatters the roof beneath her cheek with blood.

"Baby?" I whisper, touching her hair gently, moving my knife down to the bindings on her wrists. Her injured left arm is drenched with red, the bandage soaked with blood. "Can you hear me, Cross? You in there?" Just knowing she's alive sparks my body with a raging fire of relief that burns the clouds of doubt away. How this car, right here, on this day managed to get in an accident is beyond me. Coincidence, maybe? Fate? "Amy, come on, sugar. Let me know you're okay." I remove the cord at her wrists, releasing her arms slowly. A scream tears straight through her throat, echoing around the crumpled car and bringing me the worst agony I've ever felt in my damn life. "Fuck, sugar, I'm sorry." I decide against cutting the cord off her ankles. I don't want to hurt her again.

"Austin?" Amy whimpers with her bloody lips. My eyes widen as I lean over her, touching a hand to her cheek just as her eyelids start to flutter. A second later, a man is tapping on my leg and telling me to move. It's the paramedics. Sometimes strength is in doing the best you can, no matter the situation. Other times, it's knowing what you *can't* do and accepting that as truth. I pull back with a promise to follow Amy to the hospital, and let the experts do their thing.

In the back of my mind, vengeance burns white hot and painful.

CHAPTER 21
AMY

I wake up feeling quite sore, my stomach twisting and turning in my belly. I reach up to clamp a hand over my mouth and scream when pain ricochets through my body. *Oh dear.* My eyes fly open and for a second there, I'm blinded by the white lights above me, the sterile walls and floors, the flowers.

"Where ... " The word gets caught in my dusty throat and hangs there, threatening to explode from my lips along with a wave of nausea. I hold it all back with a push of strength I'm surprised to even find in me. My entire body feels like it's been run through the washer, spun this way and that. All of my muscles are sore, while half of my bones feel like they've been broken and put back together again. *What happened?* I remember

Margot kidnapping me just moments before my lovely bath and book date I had set up. I remember listening to Margot threatening Austin. I remember feeling a cold knot of fear.

I remember being pregnant.

I try to move my right hand instead of my left and am relieved when it obeys. I clutch my fingers over my belly and suddenly, something that seemed so complicated becomes simple. I *want* to have this baby. I didn't expect it, but I didn't expect Austin either. Besides, I've seen what a life looks like when everything goes to plan. It might work for some people, but not for me.

"My baby," I whisper, struggling to sit up.

"Shh, calm yourself down." I recognize that voice. My head whips to the side and my vision tilts and tumbles, forcing me to close my eyes before I get a glimpse of that familiar face.

"Mama?" I ask, fighting back another wave of nausea. "What are you doing here? Where's Austin?" I won't lie – no daughter could ever be disappointed to find their Mama is there in a crisis, even with the bad blood between us. But the person I need most in this world is Austin Sparks. I have a vague recollection of hearing his voice in that dark memory between Margot's conversation and where I'm at now. Whatever happened in between, I'm not sure, but it doesn't really matter. I'm alive, and I'm safe. As long as I've still got my baby, everything else can be forgotten.

"Don't be silly. I'm here because I'm your mother." I feel her cool hands on my forehead, sweeping my hair away from my face. When the sick feeling in my stomach subsides, I open my eyes again and find my mother standing in a shaft of sunlight. The single golden beam breaks through a crack in the utilitarian starkness of the curtains. Mama doesn't look as if anything has happened between us, as if I hadn't run away and disappeared for several months. Her mouth is set in a straight line and she looks very businesslike. "Relax for a moment before you sit up. I won't have you passing out again."

I lay my head back against the white pillows and wonder a question I'm too afraid to ask. *Is Papa here?* I clear my throat and try to decide if I feel comfortable asking my mom another question, one that I absolutely must have the answer to *now*.

"Mama, is my baby ... is my baby alright?" She pretends like she doesn't hear me, moving over to the window and pulling the curtains back. The clusters of flowers frame my mother in color, highlighting the simple elegance of her cream dress, the perfection of the folds as they drape down to her ankles, swirling gently as she turns back to face me. Her brown eyes get that purple sheen in them, drawing the breath from my lungs. I've always wondered how I turned out to be so plain Jane when my Mama is a work of living art.

She stares at me and this look I've had turned on me so many times suddenly becomes less frightening, less stern. I'm not afraid of her anymore, and that makes me feel good inside. Or it would if I had an answer to my question. I tighten my fingers against the thin material of my hospital gown.

"Mama?" I ask, and she sighs, moving over to a vase of pink roses near the door. She fluffs the bunch with her hand, pausing to adjust a blossom.

"How did you end up bound and gagged in the back of a car?" she asks and I nearly scream, tears pricking my eyes as I look up at the ceiling and pray to Sali Bend for strength.

"Don't be cruel," I whisper, wondering why she's here, why I'm not surrounded by Triple M'ers. I *need* to see Austin, and I'd love to see Tease, Kimmi, even Mireya. I was glad to see my mom, but if she isn't going to act like a mother, I'd rather she just left. "Did I lose my baby?" Mama scoffs and shakes her head, brushing a strand of cinnamon colored hair behind her ear.

"It might've been a blessing if you had," she snaps at

me, and I gasp. For a second there, she reminds me of an evil step-mother from a fairytale, like at any moment she might grow a tail an turn into a fire breathing dragon.

"That was quite rude of you to say," I whisper. I almost call her a trollop, but the words won't come through the relief. *She's okay*, I think, letting my palm lie flat against my belly. *We're both okay.* So where's Austin? I'm not silly enough to think he's left me. He would never. My best guess is that he's not *allowed* in here. I bet none of them are. "What did you say to the staff?" I ask her, but I know she's not likely to answer that question either.

"Jesus Christ, Amy," she bursts, the words exploding from her puckered lips like poison. I catch myself cringing away and berate myself for being weak. Forcing my tired, aching muscles to lift me up, I glare at her. "Bound and gagged? It's like something from a horror movie. You disappear, and I don't hear from you, and then Christy ... " Mama huffs. "You'll tell me where she is right now. Mr. and Mrs. Hall are here to collect her."

"Christy is a grown woman, as am I. If she wants to see her parents, she'll pick up a phone." Mama's lips get so tight, they turn white.

"Not if she's bound and gagged in the back of some

mafia gangster's car, she won't." I almost laugh.

"Mafia? They're bikers, Mother. At least get the terminology right." My mom steps forward, like she wants to hit me, but she doesn't. She drops her arm and freezes in place next to the hospital bed.

"You're coming home with me and your father. We'll send you away for a little while, and then you'll come back, all sins forgiven." I grit my teeth and feel my hands turning into fists. You'd think I was sixteen years old, just come off the Mayflower, a young slut in Puritanical America. Not a twenty-one year old woman with a lover and a baby on the way, a woman who survived a gunshot wound. Yes, I am very proud of that fact. I may gloat about it for some time to come.

"You expect me to say yes to that proposition?" I ask, glancing down at my left arm. It's in a sling now and since Mother doesn't seem to be in a very giving mood, I'll have to wait for a nurse or doctor to come in and tell me what's wrong with it.

"I don't expect you have a choice. Do you see your bikers here now?" She gives me a triumphant look, eyes flashing dangerously. If I were whole and well and not such a proper lady, I might've slapped her in that moment.

"I don't know what you've told the staff here, but when they find out Austin is the father of my baby, they'll let him in."

"You're nothing but a dirty, useless little slut that doesn't know the value of her own life." My mother's brown eyes fill with tears, and even though she's just insulted me, I feel bad for her. I do. She loves me, and she's worried. Understandable considering the circumstances, but if she wants me to have a relationship with her, then she's going to have to redirect her focus to getting along with me instead of simply trying to control me. "What is wrong with you? Where's the daughter I spent my life raising right?"

"Mama, please calm down," I tell her, trying to keep my voice steady and even. "Austin has been nothing but a perfect gentleman to me – " Mama interrupts me before I can finish my sentence.

"By sticking in his dick in my daughter? Over a pool table? In a *bar*?" She snaps the last word off her tongue so fast I almost get whiplash. *Oh, yes. The video.* I'd not forgotten that Mireya sent my parents Austin and my sex tape, but I'd wished to. Now, here it is, the topic of conversation. *Well, this is quite embarrassing.*

"He's the first and only man I've ever been with, and he loves me." *Even if he's never said it,* I think to myself. "And I love him. We're having a baby, Mom." She shakes her head, and I have to wonder if she's even heard a single word I've said. My mom isn't easily reduced to curse words or vulgarity, so the fact that she's using them now is a bad sign. I open my mouth to speak again when the door to the hospital room opens and my father enters. He's got a nurse with him, a nice older lady with dark hair and a gentle touch. She checks in with me first, asking some questions and monitoring my vitals, keeping me from focusing too hard on my dad.

I dread the moment she leaves the room.

"Amy," Papa says, quite pleasantly. He knows there are eyes and ears everywhere in a hospital, and I can't imagine he'd do anything to tarnish his good name. Mama stands close to him, fingers curled around his arm. I try not to look into his face, but it's so severe, much sharper than I even remember. "There are some police officers waiting outside to speak with you. As soon as you're well enough, they'd like to come in." He smiles and I look away, almost defiantly. *Fuck.* I think the word in my head, not for my parents' benefit, but because I don't want them to know how worried I am. If there's a story, something I'm supposed to say for the club's benefit, I don't know what it is. Do I implicate Margot?

"Send them in," I say, lifting my chin. *I have nothing to hide.* That's what they have to think. It's what everyone needs to think. My hope is that they're only here about the accident, that they don't ask about the gunshot wound on my left arm, or anything that's happened prior. *The murders, the gunfights, the bank robberies.* My dad smiles at me and disappears, returning with two detectives whose names I completely blank on. My mind is too busy coming up with a story.

"Margot Tempe," I tell them, deciding to leave out anything MC related in this conversation. "She was jealous that her ex-girlfriend dumped her for my best friend." I relish the expressions on all of their faces.

CHAPTER 22
AMY

After the detectives leave, my parents disappear for awhile, and I end up falling asleep. Part of me wonders if I really am tired or if I'm simply avoiding the inevitable conversation with my papa.

When I next open my eyes, the room is mostly dark, lit simply with a light glow from the machines that surround me on either side, a sea of beeping electronics that pulse in time with the beat of my heart. I'm alone for now, blanketed under a wave of blackness and draped in anonymity. *Here's my chance.* I struggle to sit up, breaking out into a sweat that sticks my hair to my forehead. It takes me awhile, but I manage, giving myself a mental high five for the effort. *Good job, sugar,* I tell myself with a small smile.

There's a white corded phone sitting on the nightstand near my bed, surrounded by flowers and obscure in all of its antiquity. While the machines monitoring my body look like something out of a sci-fi novel, this phone is practically an antique. I lean over, crying out at the pain in my side, reaching for it with questing fingers. It might only be a couple of feet away, but it feels like a million.

I pause, sitting back and taking another deep breath. One last lunge and I end up with the phone in my hand, dragging the entire base of it along with me. I put the handset up to my ear, dialing Austin's number from memory. I made a point to memorize a few of the numbers when he first gave it to me, just in case. It seems it was a skill well learned.

I close my eyes tight and wait. It only takes two rings for him to pick up.

"Austin Sparks," he barks, voice gruff and full of emotion. I tear up then. I don't mean to, but goodness, it feels nice to hear his voice. I sniffle once before answering and right away, he realizes it's me. "Sugar?"

"Austin," I whisper as salty tears leak down my cheeks. "I'm okay, Austin." I hear him growl under his breath, both cursing and thanking God for my phone call. I take a deep breath and whisper, "So is our baby."

"Amy Cross, I miss you so hard it hurts." He

squeezes the words out quickly, cursing again. I wonder where he's at right now?

"How long have I been here?" I ask him. It might've been a day, could've been a week. I have no sense of time right now.

"Four days," he says, and then, "I wanted to come see you, Amy. I've tried everyday since, but they won't let me in. Won't let any of us in. I even told 'em we were married, but I couldn't prove it, and your parents said I was a liar, that you didn't want me there. I'm not exactly as convincing as a preacher, so they threw my ass out."

"Where are you now?" I ask him, heart thudding nervously inside my chest. I don't owe my parents anything, and they certainly aren't in control of my actions, but I simply don't want to deal with them right now. If they walk in and find me on the phone with Austin, another fight might break out, and I just don't have the strength for it at the moment.

"At the clubhouse," he says, voice suddenly low and quiet. "We didn't want to risk anyone else getting kidnapped. Margot's gone, you know. Left the hospital before we even figured out what room she was in."

"It's not your fault, Austin."

"Amy," he says firmly, stopping me in my tracks. "It was my fault. I'm the leader of Triple M. It's always my fault if something happens to one of you. I don't think I've been a very good leader thus far, but I promise you, princess, that is going to change." I touch my fingers to my throat, surprised at how much this small speech is affecting me. Austin is … *hot* when he's taking control apparently. *Amy Cross*! I scold myself. *Now is not exactly the best time to be wetting the hospital sheets with lust.* "Amy, about the baby – " My turn to cut Austin off.

"No," I tell him, shaking my head even though he can't see me. "Not over the phone, not right now. Whatever it is you're going to say, I want you to say it in person." I twirl the cord around my finger, like a high school girl from decades prior, before cellphones were even invented. "I'm not in such bad shape. Now that I'm awake, I imagine they might release me in a day or two." I touch my fingers to my head. I still don't know all the details – whether I had a concussion or whatnot – but I feel okay. A sprained arm instead of a broken one, some bruising, a few cuts here and there. I don't see any reason that I should have to stay in the hospital. "You'll come here and get me?"

"I'd ride to the ends of the earth to find you, sugar." I smile and then immediately frown when the door starts to open.

"I'll call you back when I know more." I pause as

my dad's face appears in the doorway. "I love you." And then I hang up before Austin gets a chance to respond. The phone clicks gently back into place as I look up and meet my father's eyes. They're blue, like mine, but much, much darker. Perhaps the eyes really are the windows to the soul, and I'm simply gazing deep inside of his? He acts as if he's full of holy light, but all I see is darkness. Those who are truly happy, inherently divine, they don't judge others for their differences. "Papa." I say the word slowly, letting him hear the power in my voice. *I will not be swayed.*

My dad moves over to sit on the end of my bed, his best minister face fully locked in place. His dark hair is perfectly combed, and he's got on a very nice suit. It must be new because it's one I've never seen before. The air in the room smells of my father's particular scent – tobacco and cucumbers. I don't mind it; it's certainly better than the rancid sharp stink of iodine.

"Amy." His voice is the same as mine – firm, unyielding. This is a battle he already believes he's won. When he reaches out to place one of his hands on mine, I let him. If Papa were to apologize to me right now, say that he was genuinely sorry for all of the beatings, all of the moral and psychological hurt he's heaped on me all these years, I'd probably forgive him. But he won't. And knowing that is one of the hardest things of all. "I have a friend with a ranch a couple of hours outside of Wilkes. He's agreed to let you stay there for the rest of your pregnancy."

"Because having a baby out of wedlock, even if it's with the man I love, is entirely unacceptable. How will the people in Wilkes talk? What would the church think?" I put a hand over my mouth in a pretend gasp, enjoying my father's accompanying frown.

"We all make mistakes in our lives, Amy. You're young, but when you get a little older you'll realize a life like this is no life at all. Honey, you were *kidnapped*. Any why? Because two lesbian bikers got into a lovers' quarrel? Do you even hear the words that are coming out of my mouth?"

I stare him straight in the face and then switch our hands, so that mine is covering his instead of vice versa.

"I will admit that the kidnapping was not entirely pleasant, but there are risks in every life, and I've chosen this one. I accept the price. Father, a few moments of tragedy are worth a lifetime of joy. If you can't be happy for me, then we can't have a relationship. I'm sorry, but the door is always open. When you're ready to be a grandfather to this baby, I'll have you around." I release him, watching a flush of red climb his neck onto his face. This is not how he wanted this to go. He's used to controlling me, and I let him. For twenty-one years, I let him. Not anymore. I don't regret my choice.

"Don't be unreasonable, Amy. Think of your mother. She's been sick with worry, waiting for you to call her, and you never did. She's spent nearly all of the last three months crying." I don't doubt his words. In fact, if he'd said anything else I would've called him a liar.

"You and Mama might be a couple, but you're still separate people. You each have your own decision to make."

"That's not how this is going to work, Amy," my dad interjects, rising to his feet. I watch him stand. "If you say no to coming with us, you say no to having a relationship with your mother. I know you don't want that. She'll be devastated if you do this." I swallow back tears. I have to be firm with them. My whole life, my father thought to train me up as a child. Right now, I feel like the tables have been turned. As Glance Serone might say, *You'll always owe a debt to your parents for raising you. At some point, the debt has to be repaid. You can do that by teaching them a thing or two. They might be surprised to learn it, but there's wisdom in every child.* Of course, then he'd grin and probably fuck Sali over the back of the sofa, but there's still intelligence and a hint of reason in his words.

I stay firm.

"If this is what you want to do, I can't stop you, but I beg you to reconsider. Take my phone number and call me when you change your mind." Papa ignores me, dark brows drawing low over his eyes.

"Where's Christy? Her parents are worried, especially after that nonsense you told the police."

"Christy is a grown woman, Papa. If she wants to speak with her parents, she'll call them." I pause. "And she's a lesbian, Dad. And proud of it." My father's nose wrinkles and he spins on his heel, disappearing out the door and storming down the hall with as much self-control as he can muster. I relax back into the pillows, suddenly exhausted again. The emotional toll of dealing with one's family can be likened to a terrible car accident – trust me, I've been a part of both, and I can easily testify to which is more painful.

I'm about to drift into sleep when the door opens and my mother enters. She pauses at the foot of my bed while we stare at one another.

"Your number," she says, her voice clipped. Her gaze keeps flicking back to the door, as if she's afraid my father might walk in and catch her. I search around for something to write on, groaning with the movement, when she sighs and tosses a pen and a small pad of yellow sticky notes towards me. I scribble the numbers down and hand them to her, nearly jumping from my skin when she moves close and ... presses a kiss to my forehead. Without another word, my mother disappears and on my lips, is a smile.

This car accident may not be the worst thing that ever happened to me. To be honest, it might just be one of the best.

CHAPTER 23
Austin

I've spent almost a week in misery, waiting for Amy, unsure what was happening at the fucking hospital. Goddamn red tape and two holier-than-thou parents kept me from her side and put an aching hole in my gut. I've been a crazy man, I'll admit. My fellow Triple M'ers have taken to avoiding me at all costs. Today, I'm even worse, pacing the length of the bedroom like a caged bear. *No, not* the *bedroom* – our *bedroom*.

"Stop acting like a man gone mad, Austin Sparks," I tell myself, pausing to look in the mirror over the dresser. Yeah, that's right – dresser. Even though the house isn't done, I got furniture for Amy. At first it was just a bed to rest in, but then it became a nightstand, a lamp, a picture, even a fuckin' potted plant. Mr. Austin

Sparks cut a real strange figure at all the furniture and antique stores he's been visiting. Even though the employees looked at me like I was convicted murderer, walking around in my club's leather vest and my favorite boots, I managed to put together a real nice set of stuff for Amy. I might be a man, an uncouth one at that, but I had a momma that ran a bridal shop. I watched her work in there everyday after school, saw her put together a place that was every woman's dream. Girls used to gasp and cry when they walked in there. My momma knew how to decorate, so fuck anyone that doesn't like it, but I know how to decorate, too. I look around at the walls, the high ceiling, the crown molding. It's done. Finished. I wish I could say the same about myself.

I touch my hands to my stubbled face and my unkempt hair. Fuck, I smell like sweat and dirt, and don't look much better. Kimmi's probably on her way back now, sitting with Amy in our new car. Yes, *car*. It's a fucking dirty word, I know, but what am I going to do with a baby? Shit, with *two* babies? Put 'em on the back of my bike? So I bought a car. It ain't fancy, but it'll do. I wanted Amy to see more than hear, that I'm ready for this new life.

"I should've gone to the fucking hospital," I mutter, peeling off my clothes and tucking them in a clothing hamper. My grandmomma would be proud o' me. The room wasn't quite ready for Amy though; I had to finish it up. Or I keep tellin' myself that. In reality, I think I was just worried about my reaction. When I see her, I might go bat shit nuts.

I shower quick as I can, admittedly enjoying our fancy ass new bathroom, and come out to find that Amy's already sitting on the bed waiting for me. There's a look of raw wonder in her face and a discarded book lying by her side – of course.

"Austin," she whispers, looking around in awe at the pale blue and white pinstripes on the wall, the carefully hung pictures, the rug, the white sconces that frame the mirror. "What have you done?" I think the thing she notices most though is the crib. I bought a fucking crib. Who ever woulda thought, huh? "Why?" She looks like she's holding back tears, but I don't know why. This is a good moment, right?

I move towards her, nothing but a towel wrapped around my hips and bend down, putting a hand on her knee.

"This is called *I'm sorry for being an idiot, sugar.* I hope you like it." She turns to me slowly, reaching out her fingers and touching them to either side of my face. I shaved for her, so the skin on my cheeks is smooth. I hope she likes that, too. "I been actin' a damn fool,

Amy. I've always been a wanderer, you know? I didn't want to get chained down in one place or to one woman." I squeeze her knee as I'm talking, so she knows I don't mean her. "But while I was freaking out about losing that part of my life, I wasn't paying any Goddamn attention to what I was gaining." Amy slides her fingers down my face, dropping her hands to my shoulders. Her touch makes me crazy, and I can barely contain myself as I kneel there, shaking with need, desperate with desire. I want to fuck her, make love to her, whatever. I just want to be inside of her. *No, no, I need to be inside of her.* "A real man takes care of his family, Amy. Triple M is my family, you're my family, and … " I swallow hard. "This baby is my family."

Amy leans forward and kisses me, so softly that her lips feel like fabric brushing up against my skin. I ain't a poetic man, but if I were, that shit would make me write sonnets. Amy moves her mouth to my chin, kissing the freshly shaved skin there, running her tongue along my jaw bone, all the way up to my ear. I shiver and squeeze her knee so hard she jumps in surprise.

"You're hurt, baby," I tell her, my mind drifting back to that sickening moment when I found her gone, to the even worse moment when that car flipped over and I thought she might be dead. I haven't yet had a chance to deal with *The Branded Kestrels MC* extraordinaire motherfuckers, but I will. I'm just biding my time for the perfect opportunity. I haven't been much of a leader yet, but I'm going to be. I just need another chance to prove it. "We can't, you know, get down and dirty. If you keep doing that, I won't be able to hold back."

"You can't handcuff me tonight or pound me over a countertop, but I can still have sex." Amy whispers into my ear, "Nothing down below suffered any damage." Her hot breath brings my cock to full attention and my hands up to her hips, scooting her back and pulling her onto the bed beside me. I pay special attention to her left arm, making sure she's laying with it facing towards the ceiling. I press my erection into her back and run my tongue along her ear. "What are you doing?" she whispers as I pull the towel away and slide her skirt up.

"For once, you actually listened to me, Amy Cross. You really are starting to learn like a proper student." She groans and arches her back into me, letting me slip my dick between her legs and find her opening. It's hot and ready for me, spreading wide as I move slowly inside, pushing deep and pausing with our bodies locked together. "I really do hate fucking pants."

"Austin, slow down," she gasps as I reach around her body and find her clit. "It's been days, and I've been trapped in that horrible hospital with nothing to read." Amy yelps as my grip tightens and I graze my teeth over her neck. My chest presses along the length of her back, begging for skin to skin contact. I massage her for a moment more before I slide my hand up and push her shirt aside, unclasping her bra and grinding my skin against hers. She moans and rocks her hips back, spearing her body on mine and making us both gasp with pleasure. "I'm going to come already and leave you in the dust."

"That's okay, sugar, because tonight, you're going to come a lot. More than should even be legal." I thrust my hips against her ass, enjoying the softness of her cheeks as our pelvises knock together. My hand moves down her belly, and up the inside of her shirt, beneath the loose bra, and finds her tits.

"Austin, they're sore. I wasn't joking about that," she says, trying to pout her lips but failing when she ends up moaning instead. "Be gentle with them." I caress her softly, gritting my teeth at the animalistic urges that come raging through me. Gentle. I gotta be gentle. This is going to be a challenge.

I bring my hand back to her hip, holding tight as I move inside of her, enjoying the slick wetness as I glide in and out, eliciting sharp, little bursts of breath from her lips that drive me to the edge of my sanity. My fingers find Amy's clit again, circling the tight little bud and putting just enough pressure on it that her pussy clamps down on me, squeezing and throbbing and threatening to tear my cock to pieces. I might even enjoy it while it was happening. *Holy mother of fuckin' shit.*

"Come for me, baby. Just one to loosen the pressure. Then we'll move onto number two."

"Austin, stop," she says, but she doesn't sound like she wants me to stop. Amy moves her hips against mine, quickening the pace as I rub her clit in circles, bringing her to a shuddering orgasm that tears through her body and damn near cuts into mine. I clench my damn teeth and force back my release, squeezing my stomach muscles and sliding out of Amy with sheer force o' will. "What are you doing?" she asks as she lies there, all pert and pretty and vulnerable. All mine.

I scoot down towards the end of the bed and grab Amy's feet, pulling her socks and boots off and tossing them to the floor. See, this is why I like women. Her feet don't smell like something crawled in there and died – like Beck's – instead they smell soap and roses. You tell me how in the hell that's even possible.

"Quote me some more Shakespeare, baby," I whisper against the arch of her feet. I press my lips against her skin and she moans, toes curling. Tiny beads of sweat gather on her exposed back and belly, remindin' me that air conditioning is still very much on the top of my list. For the moment though, I'm gonna enjoy it. The heat amplifies the smell of sex in the room, tightening the skin on my balls and promising me one hell of an orgasm.

"Fuck Shakespeare," Amy groans, rolling onto her back and wincing. I almost go feral right there, seeing my baby in pain, but she locks her eyes on mine. "Don't you dare stop."

"Oh, you're giving me orders now, huh?" I ask, sliding my hands down her foot. I done some reading while she was gone, not a lot but a little, and I hear that pregnant ladies like their feet massaged. That, I can do. I press my thumbs into her flesh and she whimpers. From the look on her face, I figure I may as well be touching her clit. *Look at this, an untapped resource I been missin' out on all these years. And here I thought I was a ladies' man?*

"You're just as much mine as I am yours. I don't see why not." Amy lifts her chin defiantly, biting her lip when I squeeze her foot again. The hot air in the room twirls lazily, stirred up by the ceiling fan, and brushes against my dick, drawing a small groan from my throat. I grab Amy's other foot and move it down, sliding both feet against my cock. Her juices act as lube as I groan and thrust gently between them. "What are you ... Austin ... " I watch her pupils dilate and a red flush rise to her cheeks. "You're a dirty boy." Amy swallows hard as I grin big at her.

"Now, there's the nasty talk I was lookin' for." I continue to thrust slowly between her feet, pre-cum leaking out of my cock and keeping it nice and slick. Not as good as a pussy – nothing is – but it'll do.

"I am the ... " Amy swallows again and clears her throat, resting her head back into the pillows. Her right hand sneaks down between her legs and finds her clit, rubbing across it gently before sneaking inside her own wetness. "I am the future mother of your child. You should treat me with respect."

"Oh, sugar," I growl, feeling my blood pump faster and my cock swell with need. "When I'm with you, I'm happier than a tick on a hound dog."

"That's disgusting," she whimpers, but she doesn't stop fingering herself. The look on her face says it's anything but.

"And I do respect you, princess. I respect the hell out of you for putting up with a dumb ass like me." I set Amy's feet down on either side of me and crawl forward, kneeling between her legs and running my hand down my cock. We pleasure ourselves together, watching, the air between us quivering with tension. I milk my hand down my shaft, my ass clenching tight as I struggle to keep myself from coming all over Amy's breasts. This isn't about me, not today. I'll have my fun later, when she's swollen and pregnant with my baby. Then I'll let the feral male inside of me go wild. Right now, I want to see if I can get her to come in triplicate.

"Do you always celebrate big occasions with sex?" she asks me, and I pause, scooting back and grabbing her beneath the thigh. I push Amy's leg up towards her chest, so I have a nice view o' the downstairs. I stick my fingers in my mouth, coating them nice and pretty like, and then I thrust them inside, right beside hers. Our fingers mingle in her tight heat for a moment before she gives up and collapses back, her wet hand lying splayed across her belly.

"Is there a better way?" I ask and she nods. I raise an eyebrow as Amy pinches her eyes shut tight and arches her back. I slip in a third finger. "How do you figure?"

"A ride," she whispers and I laugh, curling my fingers up and searching for that sweet little spot that drives women mad. I don't rightly know why they call it a G-spot, but I figure it feels damn good, so maybe that's it.

"Sugar, unless I'm riding you, I'd have to respectfully disagree." I press my thumb into her clit, guiding it back and forth as I fuck her with my hand. Amy's pussy is already so tight, it's hard to move. I smile and hope her second orgasm is better than the first.

"Fuck me, Austin. I want you inside of me," she groans, voice hardly audible over the slick, wet whispers of her cunt. I don't stop, not even when her small hand encircles my wrist and tries to pry me away. "I need your dick."

I laugh and Amy flushes a bright red color that only does her full cheeks justice. I slap the pale flesh of her hip and try not to blow my load when it jiggles enticingly. Amy's in good shape, but she's still a curvy woman. The perfect woman. *My* woman.

"Come for me one more time, and I'll give it to you."

"Austin!"

"Amy," I breathe, quickening my pace and slamming my knuckles into her cunt. She writhes in place, reaching up and pressing the pillow against her face. Amy bites the fabric hard, rocks her hips up against my hand, and comes again, drenching my hand with her sweet juices. A sound scrapes from her throat, like an animal in heat. That right there does me in real good. Even if I wanted to, I can't wait anymore.

I slide my fingers out and reach under her ass, dragging her towards me with little effort. I press the head of my cock against her opening, feeling the warming welcomeness of her wet pussy. Sweat pours down Amy's exposed belly, dotting her tits with moisture. The nice little cream skirt she's wearing is pushed up her hips, leaving her fully exposed. I grin and thrust forward, filling her as she screams and writhes beneath me.

"I can't do it again, Austin," she whimpers, keeping her eyes shut tight. I lean over her, her leg still clutched in my left hand. But if I've learned anything these past few months, it's that Miss Amy Cross is *limber*. I press her leg towards her chest, pausing with my lips hovering just a breath above hers.

"Open your eyes," I tell her, and she does. Her lashes flutter open and those big, beautiful baby blues stare me straight in the face as I start to move. She's so wet and ready that I don't need to go slow. I let loose, pounding my body into hers, enjoying the slight breeze from the ceiling fan across my back. "Keep watchin' me, sugar," I command, keeping our gazes locked, our faces inches apart. One of Amy's hands comes up and touches my chest, feeling my skin with gentle fingers. Her nails curl against my body as she groans, sliding her touch to my tattoos and tracing them with quaking fingertips. Even though she's already mine, already marked with my seed, I bite my lip hard and come inside of her, enjoying the wide-eyed expression on her heart shaped face. My release is quick and swift, ridin' over me and drawing sounds of pure, male pleasure from my throat. I guess Miss Cross likes that, too, because she drops her hand back to her clit, rubs it hard and comes like the feral little kitty cat I know she is.

Shit, and I was worried about bein' with one woman for the rest of my life? I release Amy's leg, panting and staring down at her face. I don't pull out of her though, just sit there, locked together in body like I'm pretty dang sure we already are in soul.

"You're more woman than I'd ever hope to need," I tell her, and I hope she knows that's a compliment. Amy smiles and reaches up her right hand to brush against my jaw.

"And you," she says. "Are most certainly the only man capable of melting my panties, and decorating my bedroom. Austin Sparks, I love you like the desert loves the rain."

CHAPTER 24
Amy

I sleep straight through to the next morning, relieved to be home and thoroughly tired out by Austin's ministrations. Even thinking about it makes me flush though I'm not sure why. It's certainly not the first time we've had sex. I feel my cheeks heat, even through the redness that's already there, pulled from my skin by lazy summer warmth. Today I've dressed in leather pants, even though they're not the most comfortable item of clothing to wear. I simply want to. I had to come home wearing the clothes my mother had taken to the hospital for me. *Old* Amy clothes that look more like a tablecloth than anything else. I promptly dump them in the massive garbage can by the front door, filled to the brim with bits of old drywall.

"So you are still alive? What a shame." I spin to find Mireya leaning against the wall where the counters used to be. She smiles at me, and I can tell she's only joking. Her dark hair is swept back and mussy, peppered with bits of white dust and spotted with pink paint. I always thought she was pretty when she was made up and dressed in her best biker chick gear, but in reality, I think she's prettier right now.

I smile back.

"Have you seen Christy?" I ask, adjusting my arm in the sling. It's not broken, merely sprained, but it's still a bit sore. My head throbs in time with the saw I can hear running elsewhere in the house, but I brush it aside. I have medication for that, thank you, and I haven't forgotten that I was in a small coma. I promise myself to take it easy.

Mireya pulls a cigarette from her jeans pocket and lights up.

"Think she's upstairs with Kimmi." I raise my eyebrows and Mireya shrugs.

"Don't ask. I don't know." I close the lid on the garbage can and head up the stairs, opening doors in my search for Christy. I hear her before I see her, laughing like I haven't heard in quite some time, like the world is open and ready to be explored. My smile turns into a grin. I turn the doorknob and step into a pale pink room, smaller than mine and Austin's, but still good sized. Christy is leaning against the wall opposite me, her blonde hair upswept and her blue eyes sparkling. When she sees me, she squeals.

"Amy!" Christy practically sprints across the room and then comes to a skidding stop when she sees the sling on my arm. I throw my good arm around her neck and give her a hug. Kimmi brushes an arm across her forehead and watches us with a smile.

"You wouldn't even know you'd picked her up from the hospital yesterday. If I didn't know any better, I'd say you hadn't seen her in weeks." Kimmi steps back from the wall and looks at it with a critical eye. "At least you're back, Amy, and you can tell Christy what a disgusting color this is. I call it baby puke pink."

"It's called Lady Lip Pink," Christy corrects, moving away from me and putting her hands on her lower back. Kimmi raises an orange eyebrow.

"I've seen a lot of lady lips," she says, making us both blush. "And I've never seen any that were this color. If I had, I'd have probably called 911."

"You're disgusting," Christy says, but she says it affectionately enough.

"I don't mean to interrupt your painters' party, but I thought it might be fun if we took a walk. There's a block of shops not too far from here, and I'm desperate to stretch my legs." Kimmi gives me a look, resting one hand on the paint splattered hem of her jeans.

"Things might look casual, but we're at war." Kimmi smiles. "If you want to go for a walk, you'll have to take an entourage with you." Her smile morphs into a grin. "Go ask Beck."

I grab Christy by the hand and drag her out of there, praying that Beck isn't ... er ... occupied with Tease at the moment. I need to talk to Christy. I feel like it's important that I do. I keep promising myself that we'll spend some time together, but I never follow up on it. After the accident, which could have been much, much worse, I don't feel like I can put it off any longer. Fortunately, Beck is standing at the base of the stairs when we pass by. I grind to a stop, Christy bumping into my back, and look down at him. He grins big when he sees me.

"Well, shoot. I thought you might've come back as ghost considering I didn't get a chance to see your pretty little face yesterday, only a hell of a lot of moans and groans." I flush again, but raise my chin haughtily.

"I'll forgive your rudeness if you promise to take us on a little walk." I glance over at my bedroom door. I could ask Austin for an escort, but I don't want Christy to be the third wheel. It's probably better if we drag Beck along. "Bring Tease, and let's go for ice cream."

Beck squeezes his empty water bottle and tosses it over his shoulder. It bounces off the rim of the garbage and hits Mireya in the leg. She scowls at him, but doesn't say anything.

"I could never say no to such a lovely lady," he says, motioning us down the stairs. "Get your asses over here, and let's go."

CHAPTER 25
AMY

"Are you happy here?" I ask Christy as we hold hands, walking down the street at a leisurely pace. Beck and Tease are a good distance behind us, but I don't doubt their ability to keep us safe in a crisis. Beck is a machine, and Tease grew up with this life. I'm not worried. Besides, things seem almost conspicuously silent. I get the feeling we're not going to be dealing with any more feints or jabs – when the next wave of trouble comes, it's going to be big enough to block out the sun. That's just my guess, of course.

"Here?" Christy asks, glancing up at the abandoned houses as we walk past. "As in this town?"

"As in being with the club?" I say, glancing down at our interlocked fingers. We walked everywhere together as little girls, always holding hands. Christy is my support and my comfort, and I don't even mind if Mireya makes fun us for this. "I wasn't sure you were going to make it at first." I take a deep breath and wait for her to respond. I have to tell her about her parents soon, that they were waiting at the hospital as well. I probably should've told her as soon as I saw her yesterday, but I couldn't. In my heart, I'm afraid Christy will break down and disappear one day, head back to Wilkes and live her life in shrouded misery.

"It's hard for me," she admits, touching her free hand to her blonde hair. It's waving gently down her neck, happy to be free of the ponytail she was sporting earlier. "Much harder than it was for you, I think. You're a much stronger person than me, Amy." I squeeze her hand.

"That's not true, and you know it. Everyone has strength inside of them if they know where to look for it. Our strengths all lie in different places, some harder to find than others. You'll get there," I say and then rethink my statement. "No, you're getting there now. Or at least you seem to be. Have you always been a fan of home improvement?" Christy blushes and steps over a crack in the sidewalk, filled with weeds and clumps of grass. It's sort of pretty, in a dystopian kind of way.

"I like to see the transformation, you know. From

broken to whole again." She shrugs as if her comment means nothing. "I just found something to relate to." Christy takes a deep breath and looks over her shoulder. Her eyes find mine and her mouth opens and closes like she's about to tell me a secret. Instead she says, "I'm even starting to like motorcycles." My turn to raise my eyebrows at her.

"Oh, really?" I smile. "Kimmi Reynolds have anything to do with that?"

"You're a bitch, you know that?" she says, and she hardly stumbles over the B-word. Good for her. "But yeah, maybe. She seems like a good person." Christy bites her lip and glances over her shoulder again before leaning in and whispering to me. "Though I think there's a strong possibility that she might be a sex addict." I laugh, almost as loudly as Beck does behind us.

"You're right on the money with that one, sugar tits," he says, and both Christy and I lean into together, chuckling.

"He hears *everything*," Christy says with wide eyes and we both flush. I'm not sure what she's thinking about, but I know where my mind is. In bed with Austin. I shiver. "I'm glad you're okay, Amy," she tells me as we get to the end of the block, and the houses start to change back to normal. The lawns here are mostly green instead of brown, and the homes well kempt. Just one more block until we get to the tiny row of shops.

"I'm glad I'm okay, too."

"And your baby," Christy says and we smile sweetly at one another. When I told her I was pregnant, she freaked out a bit. In a good way, though. Christy's excited to be an auntie. "I'm glad she or he is okay, too." I grin at her.

"I doubt you'll be thinking that when I'm begging you to change diapers." Christy rolls her blue eyes.

"Oh, please. You know I'll be happy to help." She looks down at the sidewalk and smiles softly. "Personally, the idea of childbirth is quite repulsive to me, so I'm glad you're the one taking the plunge." I bump her arm playfully with my shoulder as we cross the street. We walk in silence for another moment or two before I gather up the courage to tell her.

"I know you know my parents were at the hospital, but did you know yours were as well?" Christy's face blanches, and she shakes her head. I look away from her, towards the colorful awnings and the overabundance of brightly colored flowers that pepper the sidewalk up ahead.

"Did you see them? Are they okay?" she asks, voice much quieter than it was a moment ago.

"I didn't see them personally, but my dad said they were there. Unless, of course, he was lying, but I don't think so. They wanted to take you home."

"Well, I'm not going back," Christy declares firmly, and I'm surprised by the vehemence in her voice. "Even though it's scary here sometimes," she gives me a look, "it's better to be with people who love you for who you are. Amy, the only reason I survived in Wilkes is because you were there as well. That's the truth."

"My mom took my phone number, even though my dad said she couldn't." Christy and I both go silent for a moment. We know how that might turn out if my father ever discovers she did that. "Maybe one day we can grow a mature relationship with them. I don't know that they're quite ready for that, but they will be eventually. I'm sure of it."

"If they can get over that video," Christy says, and I smack her arm, pausing outside of an ice cream parlor that looks like it's been here since the fifties. In a good way though. "I know I'm still trying to get over it."

"Oh, shush, you brat."

"But a pool table? Amy, my goodness. Those romance novels must have truly addled your brain." She grins at me as I shove her with my hip and then drag her inside the store. Today is good, positive, *normal*. I wish everyday could be this wonderful, but sometimes, fate has other ideas.

CHAPTER 26
Austin

Now that Amy's back, it feels like all my ducks are in a row. It's time to stop waiting and take action. First step is finding Margot Tempe and putting a Goddamn bullet through her head. I did the right thing before, letting her walk away from us, but now that I've paid my respects to Seventy-seven Brothers, it's time to eliminate the threat. I hate to do it, but I won't risk Amy or Kimmi or anyone else in the club. Not anymore.

I take a tight turn on my bike, enjoying the feeling of the wind pelting my body, the sun warming the leather on my back. Now that we have the clubhouse, I'm going to have to make time to go riding. It won't just be a simple part of my day anymore. That scared me before, but I feel better now. Maybe I won't take it for granted so damn much? If it's a treat more than an obligation, won't I appreciate it more? Anyway, Kimmi and I have no plans to stop robbing banks, so I know I'll get some mileage in during our runs at least.

Even though I'm enjoying the roar of the engine and the flicker of the sun on chrome, that doesn't mean this is a pleasure ride. No, unfortunately my Triple M'ers and me are on a mission. If I let the disrespect that Bested by Crows and Broken Dallas has shown me go, then I'm nothing. I'm weak in this world, and that's a death sentence. I let this stand and even if they get tired of me and disappear, I'll have other problems. I have to prove to everyone that I can be a leader.

"Can you turn off that crap and put some real music on?" Beck asks, breaking through the intercom system and cutting off *Hell Yeah* by Rev Theory. I ignore him and keep riding. He might be our new Sergeant at arms, but I'm the Pres. I make the important decisions. I grin beneath my visor, taking the next turn nice and sharp, listening to the growl of the pavement as it disappears beneath my ride.

Mireya Sawyer, bless her black, little heart, gave us some very valuable information: the location of Bested by Crows clubhouse. It's been in the same damn place for over two decades and according to her, they're quite proud of it. O' course, they don't live in theirs like we're planning to do, but hell, nobody never said Triple M wasn't an anomaly in the MC world. Heading there, we're taking a chance. I've got twenty members of the club with me and the rest are back at the clubhouse. We could be overwhelmed and end up in another firefight, but we could also get lucky and catch 'em at a time when very few folks are there. That's the hope. Like my favorite Nickelback song, *Burn it to the Ground*, we're going to flame those fuckers out of there. The goal is to give a statement that we won't be taking their crap anymore.

Here's to hopin' it works.

"You are a real son o' a bitch, Austin Sparks," Beck mutters as we swing towards our exit and hit a sea of suburban houses and pretty green lawns. Bested by Crows has their place up a long ass driveway, gated, hidden away from the world. According to Mireya, you'd never know what it was by looking at it. I ignore my friend and try to stay focused on the task at hand. The sooner we get this shit over with, the faster we get back to Amy, and that's all I really give a shit about right now.

"Guide the way, sugar," I tell Mireya instead, following behind her bike and slowing down substantially as we get deeper into suburbia, swerving around minivans and absorbing glares from narrow eyed Southern soccer moms. Mireya doesn't answer, and I can only imagine what she's thinking in her head right now. This place holds some hard, hard memories for her, and I'm proud she was even able to guide the way. "Almost there," she replies finally, taking us to a park that's nearby. We line our bikes up along the South side of the parking lot and climb off, dragging our supplies along with us. Gonna take a whole lot of gasoline to burn this fucker to the ground.

"Alright," I put a cigarette in my mouth, "Kimmi, Beck, Mireya, and I will head through the trees and scope out the place. If it looks like we can get in and get out without a bloodbath, we'll head back and grab y'all, go in the same way." We've been over the plan twice this morning, but I want to make sure everyone gets it. I'm not playin' around, not anymore.

Bishop nods, turning around to survey the others while we head off behind a children's playground – fortunately enough for us, it's empty at the moment. Nobody talks as we hike through the trees, passing through spots of shade and dappled sunlight. It's such a nice Goddamn day today. For shame that we're going to have to fuck that up.

The walk takes longer than I expect and by the time we get to where we're goin', I've got sweat rollin' down my face and soaking into the fabric of my T-shirt.

We all pause and stare at the wrought iron fencing that surrounds the building. It doesn't look like anything fancy. I'm guessing to most folks this would look like a bed and breakfast or some shit, plain as the day is long. *Huh.*

"Doesn't look like there's a damn soul here," I tell Mireya as she squints up at the building and tries to keep a straight face. Doesn't work. Her lips end up curling into a scowl and her hands clench tight at her sides.

There's not a single bike in the massive gravel parking lot. Unless they're all inside the four car garage in the back. We stand there for a bit, surveying the property and trying to determine if it really is as empty as it looks.

"Maybe they're not using it anymore?" Beck suggests, scratching the back of his head. Kimmi and I exchange a look while Mireya moves forward and starts walking along the fence, heading towards the gate.

"After two decades, they'd just abandon it? I call bullshit. Maybe we're just lucky." She picks up her pace, forcing the rest of us to follow after. I pull my gun from its holster and curse under my breath. If anything happened to Mireya while I was with her, Gaine would cut my nuts off. And you can bet your ass he'd use a rusted knife, too. I trust him enough to keep

Amy safe, so I've got to return the favor.

Mireya pauses by the gate and flicks her hand towards a plaque. It's not fancy, but underneath the address, it says *Bested by Crows Motorcycle Club*. How motherfuckin' quaint.

"Told you," she snaps, reaching up and pushing against the gate. The door swings wide, no locks, no nothing. That ain't a good sign. I put my hand on her shoulder.

"This could be a trap," I tell her, looking back at Beck. He shrugs his shoulders and gives me his best *I don't got a damn clue* look. "We can't just walk in there." Mireya purses her lips and looks me up and down. I know her hatred for Bested runs deeper than anything I could ever comprehend, but it's blinding her to good sense. She spins away from me and takes off into the parking lot at a run.

"Son of a motherfucker," I growl, sprinting after her with Beck and Kimmi right behind me. Did I mention that Kimmi decided to join us today dressed in a studded bra and four inch heels? That girl wouldn't know good sense if it kicked her in the ass.

Mireya moves quick but quiet, like a shadow dressed in her leather pants, boots, and jacket. She doesn't bother to use the element of surprise though, moving right up the steps and to the front door. That, at least, really is locked.

"Are you fucking crazy?" Kimmi growls, pausing next to her and peering in the windows that flank the door. "You want us to get shot dead?"

"There's nobody here." Mireya says this almost as if it's a bad thing.

"Well, there's furniture inside," Kimmi adds, turning back to us with a shrug. "But she's right. There's not a soul inside that I can see. Besides, don't you think they would've announced themselves if they'd seen us coming?"

"Unless they're hiding inside, expecting an ambush." I glance over my shoulder, but it really is creepily quiet here, like a ghost town. Mireya turns to face me, leaning her back against the door.

"They merged with Broken Dallas. Maybe they've finally abandoned this place?" She stares out at the parking lot and the woods beyond with a glassy gaze, like there's another time overlaid with this one. I snap my fingers in front of her face, pretty damn sure those are memories she shouldn't be allowed to delve into. At least not right now.

"You think they'd do that?" Mireya turns away and lets her dark hair fall in front of her face like a curtain. When she pulls her gaze back to mine, the memories are gone and there's nothing there but steely arrogance.

Thank God she's with Gaine now. If anyone's fairytale fantasies could melt the ice around a frozen heart, it would be his.

"It's been a decade since I was a member. How the fuck should I know?"

"Well," Beck says, lighting up a cigarette like he hasn't a care in the world, "it doesn't look like this place has been abandoned for long, if it is at all. We might just be catching 'em at a vulnerable spot." He takes a drag on his smoke. "I say we do what we came here to do and be done with it. Whether they use this place or not, word'll get around and they'll get the message." Beck starts down the few steps back to the parking lot. "I'll get the others and we'll bring the supplies up here, light this baby up like a fireworks display on the Fourth o' July." He grins and crunches across the gravel, leaving me and the girls standing on the stoop like unwanted guests.

I didn't exactly want things to come to blows, but this is almost worse. If they're not here, then where are they? And if we can't find them, what does that mean? I doubt this shit is over. If we can't come to them, eventually they're going to come to us.

"Broken Dallas' clubhouse is way out of the way. We could head there, but it's a much longer trip. I dunno if I'm comfortable leaving the group for that long." Even being away from the clubhouse this long is givin' me anxiety. Kimmi watches me muse my thoughts aloud and then shakes her head, earrings flying with the motion.

"No. I have a feeling," she glances back up at the house. "That we're not going to have much more luck there either."

"And why's that?" I ask, hoping that she's right about this. It's a fuck of a lot easier to defend your territory than it is to invade somebody else's.

"If they're merging but running under a different name, things have to change. If they pay more homage to one group than the other, it's going to start some shit." Kimmi moves down the steps, pausing in the gravel with her gaze focused outward. "I think we might have to wait for them to come to us again." She glances over her shoulder and gives me a weird ass look when she sees me smiling. "What the hell is that expression for?"

"Well," my turn to take out a cigarette, "when they do come, we'll just have to make sure they never leave."

CHAPTER 27
Austin

I let the other Triple M'ers do all the grunt work, standing back with my arms folded and my face turned up towards the sky. They kick the door in and drench the place with gasoline, soaking the place until the smell wafts out and catches on the breeze, burning my nostrils with the acrid scent. When they're done, Beck leads everyone back to me and passes over a book of matches.

"We got a line of gas around the outside, so we can start the fire from a couple of places. Thought you might want to do the honors though." I take the matches and move up towards the house, pausing about halfway across the gravel lot. I turn back and catch Mireya staring at me with an intentness that could kill.

That woman is scarier than a nun in a schoolhouse sometimes. I look down at the matches in my hand and then back up at her.

"You want the honor, sugar?" I ask, holding out my hand, palm up. Mireya looks at it for a long while, long enough that I almost drop my offering and turn away.

"Actually, yes," she says finally, stepping forward and taking the matches. She lights one immediately, holding the flame in front of her face for a moment before stepping forward and tossing it onto the line of liquid that trails down from the steps. The house doesn't explode like it does in the movies – that ain't how gasoline works – but flames do spread up the line of liquid in a flare of heat, burning quick and spreading quicker.

Mireya and I scoot back a safe distance and watch as the house of her nightmares slowly morphs into a raging ball of flames, walking out the gate only after the sound of sirens begins in the distance. Whatever is up with Bested by Crows, this has to hurt at least somewhat. You don't maintain a clubhouse and a name for two decades to give it up easily. Hopefully this will give them my message: no more fuckin' with Austin Sparks.

CHAPTER 28
Amy

Before Austin wakes up the following morning, I explore the other house. Work has finally gotten started on this one, and the fence between the two places has been torn down in favor of a single fence that wraps both properties. I certainly hope it's up to code.

I wander the halls and count off names, listing who'll be staying in what room. Austin finally laid out a finished plan, making sure everyone was happy with the arrangements. True to his word, he really is getting his shit together. I smile at Triple M'ers as I pass, opening doors and peering in at moldy wallpaper, broken windows, and even worse – an old sleeping bag and the smell of urine. I have to say, I think this house might actually be farther along in its decay than the other one.

"Goodness." I clamp my hand over my nose and slam the door to the bedroom on my left. This place has three floors, God only knows how many square feet, and fifteen bedrooms. I wonder how much it cost? I keep walking, enjoying my brief moment of solitude but hoping I'll run into Christy at some point. I want to see if she'll help me with the tiling in one of the bathrooms at the other house.

Four doors down, I make a very interesting discovery: Kimmi and Christy locking lips, bodies pressed together against the far wall of an empty bedroom.

"Oh my." I jump and knock my injured arm against the door, drawing a small gasp from my lips and jerking both of their attentions over to me. Kimmi grins wickedly, tucking some orange hair behind her ear and keeping her other hand firmly wrapped around Christy's waist. My friend on the other hand screams bloody murder, like a pack of rabid wolves are eating at her heels.

"Amy," she shrieks, eyes so wide they look as if they're about to pop out of her head. "What are you doing back here?" I raise an eyebrow, clutching my left arm and touching gentle fingers to the bandage over my gunshot wound.

"I believe I could ask you the same thing?" I bite my

lip hard and try not to laugh. If I do, Christy will never forgive me and she could very well stay a virgin the rest of her life, just out of simple spite. I wonder if this is the secret she'd been wanting to tell me? "Shall I give you two some more alone time?"

Christy yells *no* at about the same time Kimmi growls *yes*, and I just decide to hell with the whole thing and back out of there before sparks fly. I end up sitting at the top of the stairs with my book open in my lap and a smile on my face.

You never really know someone until you have them inside of you. This is the last fucking thought that occurs to me before Paul "The Raging Tempest" Wolfe thrusts his cock inside of my desperately aching pussy.

I put my finger on the passage and look up at the ceiling, trying to imagine what Austin's name would be if he were some sort of professional fighter or wrestler or whatnot. I decide Austin "The Panty Melting" Sparks would be a good choice and bury my nose back in my book.

Paul uses his massive muscles to keep me pressed into the wall, my legs bent at the knees, feet dangling in midair. I don't have to worry about holding myself up. He takes care of that for me, pinning me there with wild thrusts and rock hard biceps. I clench my fingers around the sweaty bulges of masculine pride lining his arms and

–

"Ahem." I turn my face up and find Christy standing above me, her entire face and neck, all the way down to her shoulders, is beet red. "You are a brat, and that is all I have to say." Christy marches past me, down the stairs and out the front door. I hear a laugh from the upstairs hallway and glance over to find Kimmi strutting down the worn carpet towards me. She pauses and then decides to sit next to me, slapping a massive purse down between us. It looks like it's filled with tools – hammers, wrenches, screwdrivers. I can't keep the grin off my face.

"You not only seduce my virginal best friend, but you also can't be bothered to use a toolbox?" Kimmi raises her orange brows at me and then shakes her head with a laugh. She points down at her ridiculously sparkly shoes.

"Fashion over function, my dear Amy Cross." She reaches down and starts digging through the purse's contents. "Besides, it works, doesn't it?" Kimmi continues rifling around while I watch, waiting for her to mention the make out session with Christy. She doesn't. Instead, she pulls a revolver out of her bag and wipes it down with the flowing fabric of her loose tank top. "Here." I look at the silver weapon gleaming in her hand and don't know what to make of it.

"What's this?" I ask, almost afraid to reach out and grab the gun. Almost. My curiosity gets the better of me and, almost of their own accord, my hands snatch the revolver and lay it in my lap. "Is it loaded?" Kimmi chuckles and slides the purse between her feet.

"I might be dumb, but I'm not that dumb." She digs around in her bag again and passes me a small box. When I open the top, I find bullets in it. *Oh dear.* Chills crawl up and down my spine and at first, I can't decide if they're the good kind or not. I have no clue how to use this gun, how to load it, shoot it, clean it. But I imagine if I did, the skill could come in handy. Not that I'm desperate to shoot anyone, but a lady in this life can never be too careful. "Ask Sparks to give you a lesson." Kimmi leers at me, and I blush, though only just a bit. "It's time you and Christy learned some life skills." A package of powdered donuts appears from the purse, partially squashed but still edible. Kimmi offers me one and I shake my head. "I don't know what's going to happen, but something will. It's just an unfortunate inevitability." Kimmi stuffs a donut in her mouth, covering her freshly rouged lips with powder. She must've put it on after their make out session was over.

"Did you give Christy a gun already?" I ask and Kimmi shakes her head, leaning back and putting her arms behind her for balance while she chews the donut thoughtfully.

"You scared the crap out of her, so I missed out on my chance." A grin spreads across Kimmi's face as she leans her head towards me and whispers, "But I don't think it'd be that hard to get another." She snatches her purse by the handle, stands up, and disappears down the stairs, leaving me alone with Paul, the sexual tempest/street fighter. As deliciously juicy as he is, I much prefer my real life book boyfriend.

I close the cover and touch my fingers to the perfectly crisp and painfully detailed abdomen on the front, smiling as I stand and tuck it under one arm. With my other hand, I hold the revolver, loosely and pointed at the floor. I sincerely hope I don't spook any of my fellow Triple M'ers into shooting me on accident.

I head back to Austin's and my room and find it empty. I look around for a place to stash my new weapon and decide to put in the nightstand on my side of the bed. When I think of possible scenarios where I might require a weapon of some sort, this seems like a good option. My book goes back on the shelf, the beginning of a new collection that I hope spills over into the room and overwhelms me with dusty literature. Someday soon I'll get an eReader, but for now, the crispness of fresh pages and the smell of ink is enough for me.

I leave the room again to search for Austin and end up running into him in the hallway. Seeing him span the narrow space ahead of me causes my breath to catch in my throat and my heart to pick up speed, thudding sharply against my ribcage. Every time I see him, it's like we're meeting for the first time again. Hormones rush to fill my blood with lust, wetting my panties and turning my lips into a round 'O'.

Austin chuckles at me and lifts his fingers, brushing them over my lips as I sigh with pleasure.

"Where ya been, doll baby?" he asks me, and I swear on the Wicked Witch of the West that I nearly melt. Unconsciously, I find myself rising to my tippy toes, face tilting back, fingers splaying open against Austin's wide chest. He slides one arm around my waist and puts the other on the back of my neck, guiding our mouths together for a sensual kiss, one that's a lot hotter and wetter than I'd like to have standing in the middle of the hallway like this.

"I found Christy and Kimmi making out," I whisper and his belly laugh rumbles through me, straight down to my toes. I kiss him again, sliding my tongue across his, tasting the man, the mystery that is Austin Sparks. *I can't believe I have his baby inside of me*, I think and feel a tightening in my belly. It's quite embarrassing if you think about it. Austin came inside of me and now I'm pregnant. Yes, yes, it's biology, but it doesn't feel so scientific when you're the one it's happening to.

"Damn. You sure it's summer? 'Cause it feels like fuckin' spring." I laugh, letting Austin hold me tight against him, enjoying the strong feel of his arms. When we're standing like this, it feels like nothing in the world could hurt me. Not a gunshot, not a tornado, not a crazy biker with a crow on the back of his jacket. I grin and close my eyes, savoring the feel of Austin's hot breath on my neck as he bends down and presses another kiss to the hollow of my throat. "God," he growls, and I shiver. "If you weren't already pregnant, I might have the mind to get you pregnant again." Austin backs me up against the wall.

"What are you doing?" I whisper, trying to peer around his shoulders and make sure nobody's going to come up the stairs and find us in a compromising position.

"We're spending quality time together," he groans, grinding a very hard, very insistent erection against me. I clutch at his shoulders and think about the shops I saw near the ice cream parlor. There's one in particular I'd like to take Austin to. I tap his shoulders, trying to keep him from pushing my skirt any further up my hips. "Another skirt. Hot damn, sugar, you gonna spoil me with easy access.

"Austin, I want to take you somewhere," I say as I hear his zipper sliding over the tracks. A moment later, my panties are pushed aside, and I'm biting my lip to keep from crying out as his cock fills me up, slamming my ass into the wall. *Just like Paul "The Raging Tempest" Wolfe.* Ah, how life mimics literature. "On a date, Austin," I whimper as he grunts, thrusting into me again and turning my bones to jelly.

"In a minute, baby. We'll go wherever you want to go." I lean my head against him, wrapping my left leg around his body, feeling his pants sag below his ass, leaving his cheeks bare. I rub the skin of my calf against them, praying to God above that we don't get caught by Christy or goodness, even worse, *Beck.* I'll never hear the end of it.

"Better be longer than a minute," I whisper, feeling my ass scrape against the freshly painted wall. "Or we won't be going anywhere." Austin laughs, but he doesn't stop grinding into me, burying his body inside of mine. His moans of pleasure bring some of my own and soon we're just a sweaty, writhing mess. Fortunately for me, Austin keeps it going longer than a minute, long enough for me to come hard, groaning ridiculously loud and opening my eyes to find Gaine staring at the two of us in horror as he steps out of his bedroom.

Oh well. At least it wasn't Beck.

CHAPTER 29
AMY

With my skirt firmly back in my place and my thighs aching with the recent memory of Austin's pulsing cock, I've got his hand wrapped in mine and we're walking down the street together, just me and him. This doesn't happen often enough, believe it or not. Being the President of a motorcycle club is not an easy job, and the hell we've been through lately, plus the construction on the houses, has taken up a lot of Austin's free time. We seem to find plenty of spare moments to have sex – such as the one that just occurred – but otherwise, moments like these have been few and far between.

I enjoy the firm feeling of his fingers wrapped around mine, tangled together in a delicious mixture of hard and soft. I pull our fists up to my lips for a kiss, and he smiles at me.

"I haven't been on many dates in my life, sweetness. I can't lie about that." Austin looks down at me, his sandy blonde hair moving gently around his face in the afternoon breeze. The tiny scar on his mouth makes his smile just the slightest bit crooked, and I must admit, it might just be the most adorable thing I've seen in my entire life. "Where are we going anyway?" he asks, glancing around us with a casual air belied only by the intensity in his brown eyes. He's on the lookout, ready to protect us from whatever threats should arise. Fortunately, on this day, there haven't been any. Everyone keeps thinking something terrible is coming, but since it isn't here yet, I'm going to enjoy the day with my ... I pause. What is Austin exactly? My boyfriend? Seems too immature of a term. Lover? Too casual. He's going to be the father of my child, my first and only love. I have no clue what to call him. I leave that problem alone for now, but tuck it away to bring up later.

"If I tell you now, you may decide to turn tail and run." I enjoy the look of confusion on his face and keep walking, pulling him past the ice cream parlor and over to a shop I didn't have the guts to go in the other day, especially not with Christy. Her entire body would've been covered in a blush, and her eyes might've popped straight from her head.

"The hell is this?" Austin asks as we pause in front of a black storefront with tinted windows, boas wrapped around the throats of half-naked mannequins. I clear my throat and move aside for a couple covered head to toe in tattoos. The girl winks at me as they pass and gives Austin an approving glance. I look over at my biker boy, standing tall and gorgeous next to me, tattoos gleaming on his muscular arms, one blonde brow raised in question.

"This, my dear Austin," I say, pressing another kiss to his knuckles. "Is a sex shop." I drag him in the door before he can think about an escape route and pause, overwhelmed by the purple walls and the racks of lingerie. On one side there's a counter with a petite blonde lady behind it, organizing a shelf full of colored wigs. Behind her, an entrance to the *Back Room. Naughtiness Abounds. 18+ Only*. I try hard to keep the grin off my face, but it doesn't work. One moment, I'm drowning in naughty possibility and the sense that what I'm doing must somehow be inherently wrong, and then I'm smiling maniacally, like Beck during a fistfight.

"Holy fucking stars," Austin breathes as I break from his hand and explode into the store like a man in the desert, long denied water. *Oh yes*, I think as my fingers brush across lingerie. I hardly even look at it. Lacy panties are nice – most especially when one has long since been reduced to very tasteful, very dull, laceless, nude undergarments – but what I really want to see is in the *back*. "Sugar?" Austin asks as I wonder how this store has survived so close to the Bible Belt, and decide I don't give a *shit*, thank you very much.

"Back here!" I call as I push past a blow up doll, flushing when my hand brushes against her plastic breast. When I emerge into the other room, my jaw drops and my heart skips a beat. There are glass shelves on most of the walls, lined with cocks. Cocks, cocks, cocks. Everywhere. Glass cocks, silicone cocks, cocks that look so real, they could easily be mistaken for the real thing. In the center of the room are bins filled with condoms, bottles of lube, lotions. All of this is interspersed with random other bits of naughty – strap ons (Christy and Kimmi come to mind), whips, pornography, candles, *butt plugs*. I snort and snap a hand over my mouth.

"Oh my." The words press into my palm as I stand there with chills crawling across my skin. My eyes are so wide, they start to water in the cool blast of the air conditioning. My Mama would slap my face if she knew that I was in here, and Papa? Oh goodness. He'd most likely get the belt.

"Amy," Austin growls, coming in behind me and

curling his fingers around my shoulder. "You naughty, little bitch." I shiver and turn to face him, trying not to curl myself into his arms and beg for a repeat of earlier. Yes, the shop has enhanced my libido. This is true.

"Don't," I whisper fiercely at him. "You're going to make me crazy if you keep doing things like that." Austin stares down at me with his brown eyed gaze, his mouth quirked in a wicked half-smile. "Be a gentleman while you're in here." I cough and put my fist against my lips. "Let the beast out later."

"What if I want to let the beast out *now*?" I swallow hard and force myself away from him, putting some much needed space between us. I turn away and pretend to be interested in a bin of condoms when all I really care about are the … cocks. I just want to touch one. One of the fake ones, that is.

"You need to learn some self-control," I say, pretending I actually believe what I'm saying. "When the baby comes, you'll have to know there's a place and time for this sort of behavior." Austin comes up behind me and cups my ass, *hard*, scooting past me and pausing next to a glass shelf full of vibrators. *I* need *one of those*, I think as I watch Austin pick one up and turn it on. The pink tip whirls in a wild circle while Austin's blonde brows rise up and a laugh bursts from his throat.

"Is there anything I can help you with?" a woman

asks, coming up behind me and making me jump. I turn to face her with my hand splayed against my chest and try not to blush.

"I ... um. I'm not sure." The woman smiles at me, pushing some brunette hair away from her face. I don't miss the way her eyes swivel over to Austin and take in his tattoos and his leather vest with interest. I resist the urge to turn her face forcefully back to mine. I suppose I'll have to get used to women looking at Austin Sparks. He is quite lovely, I'll be the first to admit.

"Are you looking for a vibrator? A dildo? I've got some new porno titles in that seem to be a big hit with couples." I feel another blush creeping up my neck, and I can't decide how to answer that question. How blatantly she discusses the tools of the trade. If I could only be so bold ...

"I think we're just browsing for now, thank you," I say as I back towards Austin and turn around to find him with a whip in hand. He waves it at me and then reaches around and smacks me on the ass with it. I slap his hand away. "You're taking this better than I thought," I tell him, wondering if he's ever come into a place like this with someone else. Mireya, maybe? "Do this often?" Austin hangs the whip back up and switches his focus to a shelf full of glass dildos, gleaming in the soft lighting of the shop.

"Not once," he says, and I let out a breath I didn't even know I was holding. "But shit, sugar, this is turning out to be quite the interesting little date here. I always knew you were a kinky bitch, but this here's on a whole new level."

"You ... like it?" I ask, almost afraid of what he's going to say. I *want* him to like it because, well, *I* like it. Austin turns to face me, stepping forward and putting his hands on my hips.

"Amy, don't worry about what I like or don't like. I want you to be yourself." Austin pauses. "Even if who you are is a slutty little Southern belle." I pretend to slap his face, resting my palm gently against his cheek. "What is it that you wanted to get here that I can't give you at home?" he asks with a wink. I open my mouth, letting my eyes slide over to the vibrators.

"To be honest, Austin. I'm perfectly happy with everything you've given me." I try not to blush again. That would be a bit overkill, I think. "But I want ... all of it." Austin follows my gaze.

"All of it?"

"I want to try it all," I whisper, looking back at him. "And you're supposed to teach me. You promised."

CHAPTER 30

Austin

"I can only teach what I know," I tell Amy, gaze getting stuck on this, that, or the other thing. There is a *lot* to look at in here. *Shit on a stick son of a bitch.* I'm standing in a *sex* shop right now. Didn't even know there were so many interesting little add-ons. I've been quite happy with the base package thus far in life.

Amy slides her hand away from my face and tucks some of that silky chestnut hair behind her ear. My fingers twitch as I not only imagine but specifically recall wrapping my fist in it and pullin' hard. I have to swallow back a wave of lust. While it might be okay to walk around a place like this with a hard-on, the girl tidying up the shelves is givin' me nasty looks. I'd rather not give her a reason to stare at my junk.

"Then I guess we'll learn together," Amy coughs out, voice rough as she skitters away from me, moving just out of my reach and stopping next to a display of handcuffs. *Oh, Lord above, hell yes.* I step up behind her, rubbing my body along her back but keeping my hands to myself. The sharp intake of breath that slides between her pearly pink lips makes me growl into her ear.

"Think we'll take one of these," I say, snatching a box off the wall and sliding past Miss Amy and her suddenly tight lips. She glances over at me with her sharp as shit blue eyes. I grab a candle, too. A pink one. Not sure exactly what I'm going to do with it, but when Amy smiles at me, I decide I'm on the right track. "And this." I grab the pink vibrator with the twirly thing on the top. Doesn't look a damn thing like a dick to me, but maybe that's the point?

"Are you interested in penetration or vibration or both?" the sales lady asks, appearing by my side like a ghost. The whole movement sort of reminds me of Kent, and I have to do my best not to scowl. When he did shit like that, it was like watching an arch villain vampire materialize in thin air. To be fair, this woman is a lot less scary, like a sidekick instead of a nemesis or something.

"Darlin', I ain't interested in either." I nod my chin

over at Amy. "But my baby mama probably would prefer vibration." I look over at Amy and find her biting her lip again. The look in her eyes is gentle though, loving. I don't ever want to lose that expression. The day I do is the day I'm a dead man, in the heart at least if not the soul. "She gets plenty o' penetration at home."

"Austin Sparks!" Amy scolds, coming over to stand next to me and snatching the pink vibrator from my fingers. She puts it back on the shelf. "First off, that's the *display* model. Second, this nice lady here doesn't want to hear about our sex life." The woman waves her hand dismissively.

"Wouldn't be the first or last time I'd hear all the sordid details. You would not believe what information some people will share." The woman adjusts her tank top, no longer interested in checking me out, but focused more on Amy now. "So vibration then? During intercourse or just when the man's out of town?" I let out a bark of laughter, holding up my hands and stepping back. I'll let Amy handle this part of the conversation. She gives me another look as I move towards the entrance that leads to the front of the store.

"You get whatever you want, sugar." I set the candle and the handcuffs down on the countertop. "But make sure you get this crap, too." I smile wide. "I'm going to pick you out something to wear."

CHAPTER 31
AMY

Austin and I return to the house with an oversized black bag, bulging with goodies. I make him carry it past the Triple M'ers working in the front yard and pretend I don't hear the whoops and the catcalls. They happen often enough anyway that I'm learning to block them out. But I'm still not willing to carry a heaping bag of sex toys past a bunch of rough around the edges biker folk.

Gaine's standing in the entryway when we walk in, eyes immediately catching on the bag swinging in Austin's grip. I don't look at him either – it's not easy knowing he caught us doing the naughty not an hour or so previous. *The Walk of Shame is something that should never exist because if you're shamed by what you're doing, why the hell are you doing it*? More Sali Bend wisdom to wrap around my body as I ignore the raised brow and the curious brown eyes that follow us up the stairs.

I don't know what I was expecting when I took Austin to that shop, but I don't think it was this. I guess I assumed we might buy a vibrating cock ring or something, a small trifle or token to play around with. I had no clue he'd buy me a vibrator, some handcuffs, and a silicone dildo – in *purple*.

"You're a saint among men," I tell him as we step into my beautifully decorated bedroom. My eyes catch on the crib and my fingers trickle across my belly. I threw up this morning before I went exploring, but only once. And I took four more pregnancy tests, just to be sure. So while the morning sickness is getting better, I am most assuredly quite pregnant. I touch my hands to my face and turn to look at Austin as he closes the door behind me.

The window is open, sunshine streaming through the light lacy curtains that Austin hung for me. Birds chirp cheerfully, mixing with the background noise of shovels, saws, and hammers.

"Thank you for carrying those. I didn't particularly want to drag them past Gaine." Austin tosses the bag on the bed, and then grins wide at me.

"You're worried about what that son of a bitch thinks? After he and Mireya got caught nailing each other in a stairwell at a hotel by a couple of ol' folks? Shit. And this is the same guy that put a badger down his pants to win a bet in gym class. Ignore that stupid ass." The lock on the door clicks into place a split second second before Austin's rubbing up behind me, showing me exactly how he feels about our day thus far. His erection grinds against my lower back, teasing me mercilessly. *If he doesn't stop that, I'm going to pull on his Prince Albert piercing, and quite roughly, too.* Who am I kidding anyway? Austin would probably like that.

"We should probably go help with the demolition on the second house," I tell Austin, even though my voice cracks when I say it. Austin's hands grip my elbows as he leans in and kisses my neck.

"We should probably do whatever the fuck it is I say we're going to do. Otherwise, I won't be able to think straight. Might even knock down the wrong wall on accident with this thing." Austin presses more firmly against me. "Now, open that bag and pick your poison."

"Dear God, you're insufferable," I say, but I moan while I do, so it's not nearly as believable as I'd like it to be. Austin steps back just enough that I'm able to form slightly coherent thoughts, scooting onto the edge of the bed and pouring out our dirty devices en masse. I rifle through them, perfectly aware that Sparks is staring at me while at the same time opening up his pants. His dick springs free, the piercing in the head of his cock glimmering in the sunshine. I push a few of the boxes aside and grab the dildo. It's a bold choice, but I once read a scene where the hero fucked the heroine's mouth with one while he took care of the downstairs. I cough and put my fist to my lips. I have such rancid thoughts, I must've been doomed to hell from the very start. *Now how on earth do I say this to Austin*? We're lovers, yes, but we're still working through this strange in-between phase where some things are comfortable and easy while others are still ... awkward.

I start to open the package, ignoring the little growls that are escaping his throat as he strokes himself. Now all I need to do is figure out how to phrase the question: *Dear Austin, might you be able to thrust this bit of rubber into my mouth while you pound my pussy*? I frown. This is not going to be an easy subject to broach, but I've been thinking about it for awhile now. Romance novels will do that to a person. Besides, this is the closest thing to a threesome I'll probably ever get. Not that I particularly *want* another man in the bedroom with us, but Austin would never allow it.

"Lay on your back and fuck yourself with it while I

watch," he snarls, and I nearly jump out of my skin, clutching the toy to my chest as I glance over my shoulder at him. Austin is playing with his piercing now, enjoying the look on my face as I stare at him with wide eyes.

"I'll need to lube it up first," I whisper, enjoying the way he grits his teeth and shoves his jeans violently down so that they hit the floor around his booted feet. I stand up and move over to Austin, trying to be coy. It's still a skill I'm working on. I touch my fingers to Austin's arm, kissing his bicep and the mouth of one of his skull tattoos. I slide my tongue across his skin, tracing the lines of ink that decorate his body. I bring my other arm up and show him the purple curve of our new toy. "Maybe you could lube it up for me?" I ask sweetly. "We seem to have purchased everything but that at the store." I fight back a blush. There's no need for that here, right? I reach the toy up and touch the head of my silicone cock to Austin's smoothly shaved jaw.

"Christ, woman," he says, grabbing my wrist and slamming my body against the front of his. His dick presses into my belly and I bite my lip. "You trying to put a dick in my mouth?" I laugh, even though I don't mean to.

"You won't suck it for me?" I ask with a pout.

Austin raises both his blonde brows at me.

"Sugar, the only one in here that's going to be doing any sucking today is you."

CHAPTER 32
Austin

I pull Amy to the floor, trying to be gentle with her injured arm and all that. I don't really have any fantasies of sucking on a rubber dick, but if Amy really wanted me to, I just might. *Dear Jesus, what the hell would Beck do if he ever found that shit out?* Anyway, since I'd rather not, I try a different technique to distract her. Amy is quite the dirty little kitty cat, and I bet my dignity on the fact that she'll be happy with most anything creative I can come up with.

I stand back up and look down at her, stroking my dick with tight fingers, coaxing pre-cum from the tip and holding my hand out for the dildo. Amy passes it up to me diligently. I slide my fingers down the toy, coating it with my seed, and then I give it back to her.

"Fuck yourself with this while you suck me off," I command, enjoying the feeling of taking control. Amy likes it, too. Her pupils dilate and her hand comes up, replacing my hold around the length of my shaft. She wets her lips and spreads her knees apart, reaching down with her uninjured arm and groaning as she finds her sweet spot. I watch her carefully, forcing myself to stay still while she slides the dick inside of herself. "Does that feel good, baby?" I ask as she squeezes her thighs together and sits up fully, using both hands to caress my hips, my pelvis, my balls.

"Not as good as you," she whispers, leaning forward and licking the entire length of my shaft, from the head of my cock all the way to my sweaty body. I used to think a blow job was just a blow job, but Amy Cross, little virgin Southern girl, is the best I've ever had. Hands motherfuckin' down. I groan and tangle my fingers in her hair, not pulling, not yet, just enjoying the silky texture against my skin. When I do that, she moans, too, and the vibration tingles through my dick, straight up into my brain. That poor motherfucker is already fried to shit and we just started.

Amy licks me up and down, like a Goddamn ice cream cone, pausing with her lips against the head of my cock. One hand circles my dick nice and firm, guiding my cock around her mouth, tracing the lines of her pink lips with my piercing, like she's puttin' on makeup or some shit. Amy teases my balls while she does this, tugging them gently downwards, igniting a fast burning flame that burns away some of my self-control. I'd like to grab the back of her head and fuck the shit out of that pretty, little mouth, but I don't. I am a gentleman here, first and foremost. *Fucking Christ.*

"Austin," Amy whispers, her breath cool against the slickness of my cock. "Can I try something else?"

"You aren't trying to fuck my mouth with that thing again are you?" I ask and she laughs, sending another wave of vibration into my dick.

"No." And then she's pulling away. I keep her still with my hands in her hair.

"You keep that toy inside of you, sugar. If it falls out, you're getting a spanking." Amy shivers, and I'm not sure that was much of a threat, but that's alright. Our bedroom is full of idle threats, the kind that sting whether you listen to 'em or not. I take control of my dick back, pumping hard and fast, squeezing tight, while I watch Amy struggle to crawl over to the bed with the dildo still stuck up inside of her. I hate to admit it, but I'm almost jealous of that fuckin' toy, ready to tear it out and toss it across the room, reclaim her pussy as my own.

Instead, I keep myself still, ready to try whatever Amy wants to throw my way. She is the Queen of the Blow Job, after all. I watch as she opens another package, pulling out an ugly white vibrator that looks more like something my momma might've put on her feet at the end of a long work day than it does a sex toy. It's just a stupid plastic wand with a round circle on the end.

Amy bites her lip and whimpers a little as she crawls towards the wall and plugs it in. She glances back at me and flicks a switch. A whirring sound cuts through the room as the vibrator gets going, buzzing sharply in the quiet afternoon. Amy comes back to me just in time, taking hold of my cock before I lose it and chase after her. I have no idea what she's got planned for this weird ass toy of hers – she picked it out when I was hunting down some lingerie – but I'm excited to find out.

Amy's lips close around the end of my cock, sliding forward, taking me in inch by careful inch. I get all excited, my heart pumping so fast it feels like I could very well have a heart attack right now and die happy. But then at the halfway point, she pulls back, taking a breath and starting over again. It's almost painful to watch her from above like this, see my dick disappearing down her throat.

"Fuckin' stars, sugar," I moan, letting my head fall back. The vibrator is still clutched in Amy's right hand, buzzing away but useless as a bucket of water in a monsoon. I close my eyes, enjoying the slow press of her mouth, her hot heat suctioning tight around my dick. *Heaven, pure fucking heaven.* I got the mother of my child on her knees in front of me, and she doesn't just give good head, and she isn't just a hot lay, but she also loves me. Me. This stupid, hardheaded, flighty, piece of shit asshole that I am. She loves me, and she's told me so straight, and I ain't never repaid the favor.

Fuck.

"Amy," I start, opening my eyes and looking down just in time to see her deep throat my entire shaft. This might not be the most romantic moment in the world, but I wanted to say it when it felt right to say it, and shit, this is it. Not exactly the best story to tell to friends and family, but it's raw and open, and that's what I'm gonna do.

Amy lifts the vibrator up to her face and presses the end of the wand against her cheek.

"Fucking Christ!" I scream, pulling her hair hard, my hips bucking uncontrollably as I come, shooting my load deep inside her throat. The vibration from Amy's ugly ass toy unravels me from head to toe, and I end up stumbling back, shaking and sweating and hornier than a hound dog in heat. "The hell you learn to do that?"

Amy flicks the switch on the vibrator, setting it gently on the floor and wiping her lips daintily with the fabric of her T-shirt. Her skin is pink all over, and her eyes rimmed with dark desire, hooded with lust. She stares up at me with her blue eyes.

"From a book."

Alright, that's it. I'm done being a gentleman. I stalk forward, lift Amy up under the arm pits and sweep the rest of the shit we bought onto the floor.

"Lay back, Miss Cross, and I'll teach you a thing or two."

CHAPTER 33
Amy

"Like what?" I ask as Austin reaches down and slides his hands up my belly. He rips my shirt off and grabs a black lacy bra from the floor.

"Like what turns me into a fucking madman. Put this on." He gives me a pair of panties, too – a *thong*. I stare at the bits of fabric like I've never seen the likes of them before. Me, Amy Cross, wearing lingerie? It's such an odd thought. I try not to let out any nervous laughter.

"I think I just figured that out, didn't I? Did you like the vibrator?" I smile when he growls, ripping his pants off but leaving his boots on. Oh, and the shirt comes off, too. There he is, Austin Sparks in all his glory, cock still wet from my saliva, the Triple M tattoo on his hip stark against his tense muscles.

"You can't do that to a man, not when he's about to say *I love you*."

I freeze, like a deer caught in the headlights of my daddy's truck.

"What?" My voice is a whisper, my body a string, pulled so taut I can't even breathe. It doesn't help that my pussy is clenching tight around the dildo, still stuck deep inside of me, grinding against my sweet spots when I move.

"You can't just spring that crazy shit on me when I'm gearing up for the biggest moment of my fucking life." Tears come then, even though they're silly, even though this is such an arbitrary matter in the scheme of things. Austin does love me, I know that. And I love him. And we're having a baby together, so why does this matter so much? But it does. It really, really does. "Amy," he says, stepping closer, touching his fingers to my chin. Our eyes meet, and even though he's naked and erect, and my body is quaking with need, filled up but wanting more, I find myself thinking *this is quite romantic*. Our moment doesn't occur in a candlelit grove or during a fancy dinner at a French bistro, or on the top of the Empire State Building at midnight, but it does happen. It happens so fast that I don't even realize what's going on at first, that our souls are twining and twisting into one, binding us together forever. Romance isn't defined by the place or the time or even the words that are spoken, it's defined by the feeling, the sense that you would do anything – *anything* – for this person and that they'd do anything for you.

I finally find my own words, separate from my books, from Sali Bend, from my mother. My words. Mine. To go perfectly alongside my Austin and his.

"I love you, Amy Cross. I think I have from the moment I first met you. I was just too stupid to realize it, too scared to care this much, try this hard. But I'm gettin' my shit together, and I promise you this: as long as I'm alive and breathing, I will fight through fire to be with you. I will climb mountains." Austin uses his thumbs to wipe the tears from my cheeks. "I will ride through deserts." He pauses and tries to smile at me. My body clenches tight around the toy, wishing it were him in there instead. "I'll even suck on your weird ass purple cock, if that's what you want."

I close my eyes.

"I'd do the same for you," I tell him. And then I open my eyes back up and wrap my arms around his strong neck. "I love you more than I can possibly say, but I'm going to try." I lean in close, squeezing my thighs together. Austin, God bless his heart, reaches down and cups my ass in a firm grip. "I love you like the stars love the sky, like the moon loves the sun, like the daylight loves the night. You twist my insides into knots, curl my toes, and take my breath away." I smile. "You make me want to spout poetry and quote Shakespeare, say things meant solely for the pages of greeting cards." I kiss his mouth softly. "You make me comfortable enough to want to be myself."

"Alright, that's it." Austin uses his other hand to cup me between the thighs. "Enough of this lovey shit. At least out loud anyway. If we're going to continue, let's use body language." I groan as his fingers find the toy, sliding it out slowly and then pushing it all the way back in. I bite my lip. "Put your bra and panties on for me?" I nod as Austin drags the dildo out and steps back.

"Keep it," I say before he has a chance to toss it on the floor, put it in a drawer, whatever. It's ... covered in my juices, so I'm not quite sure what the appropriate place might be. I swallow hard. After a heartfelt confession like that, how can I ask such a dirty thing? Well, because my name is Amy Cross, and I read romance novels – *proudly*. I don't care if a hundred people hear me snort with laughter, flush at the embarrassing connotations of black and white words, or flash naked men on the front covers of my reads. Fine literature can only be defined by how hot the sex scenes are. Well, at least in my book. "I want you to put it in my mouth." I don't even blush when I say it. Instead, I take a step back, drop my skirt to the floor and proceed to strip off my very tasteful, very dull, laceless, nude undergarments.

"You are one crazy chick," Austin says, lounging on the bed in the pillows, one hand behind his head, the other wrapped around the toy. "But that's why I love you." He pauses. "Fuck, that was a whole hell of a lot easier than I thought." He watches me change into the thong and the push-up bra with a hooded gaze. "Can you ever forgive me for not saying it sooner?"

"I can forgive a lot of things," I whisper, looking down and admiring the way my skin seems to glow with a pearly light, framed beautifully against the dark lace of the bra. I turn and take a nervous glance at myself in the mirror. Gone is the girl with the dull brown hair and the boring eyes, a girl whose father once compared her to a placid lake with no clouds to mar its stillness. Today, with my eyes rimmed dark with lust, my lips full and swollen, my hair mussed, I look positively *wild*. I make a sexy expression with my face, and I don't feel like a child anymore. This time, I feel like a *woman*.

I turn back towards Austin and saunter towards the bed – never previously having sauntered before, I think I do quite a lovely job at it. When I get close enough,

Austin grabs me around the waist and pulls me to him, kissing me full on the lips and sliding on top of me, his hard muscles brushing across my soft skin. When he looks down at me, I know there's not a single other place in this world that I'd rather be.

CHAPTER 34
Austin

Amy lies beneath me, a goddess if I've ever seen one. Her chestnut hair spills around her heart-shaped face, framing a beauty that's almost unreal. Maybe it's because I have feelings for her, because my heart swells when she walks into the damn room, I don't know, but I can say without a doubt that she's the most attractive woman I've ever seen.

"You sure you want this?" I ask her, holding up the toy. Amy bites her lips and looks away meaning, yeah, she does. Even if she's almost too embarrassed to admit it. I take the toy and slip it between her lips, surprised at how tight my muscles clench when I watch it disappear down her throat. I start to pump the dildo in Amy's mouth, enjoying the way her eyes flutter as she tastes her own juices, moaning as I fuck her hard with it. I position myself to slide into her, letting go of the toy and grabbing her hips. "You are such a dirty, little girl, aren't you, Amy Cross?" I ask as I thrust deep, filling her completely. Amy uses her own hand to tease me with the toy, sliding it out of her mouth and flicking her tongue across the tip. She caresses it so lovingly, sucking it deep again, tasting it with a moan, that I get jealous, ripping the damn thing from her grip and sending it flying across the room.

"Austin Sparks!" she groans in pretend outrage, raising her hips to meet me. "I think you broke a vase." I lean down and growl against her ear.

"You can use toys all you want, but I want you to remember how much better I feel."

"Oh, God, yes," she breathes, sliding her legs around me. I sit up, thrusting my hips hard, enjoying the scrape of her panties as they caress my cock with every stroke. I didn't bother to take them off – this here's half the fun. Amy's full breasts jiggle, barely trapped in the lacy darkness of her new bra. I like the look of it so damn much that I have half a mind to throw out all her other stuff and cram the drawers full of this. Lace is a mighty, mighty fine invention. "You feel so good, Austin," she whispers, making me grit my teeth just to hold back the rush of hormones. I feel like I could come a hundred times and stay hard. There just isn't enough time in the world to make me feel like I'm finished with Amy Cross. I feel like I could fuck her forever and be happy every second of it.

"I want to see you above me," I tell her, deciding to switch our positions. I pull out with a grunt and roll onto my back, taking Amy's hips as she straddles my belly, reaching down and guiding my cock back to its rightful place in the universe. She takes me in fully, right down to the last inch, sitting on my hips with her lip stuck between her teeth and her eyes half-lidded. "You're the most beautiful woman I've ever seen in my damn life," I tell her, deciding that a truth like this is better out in the open. Amy smiles as she starts to move, dipping her hand into her panties and finding her clit. I know the moment she makes contact because her entire body clenches tight around mine, squeezing me so hard it's like she's just begging me to come inside of her.

My fingers curl into the bedspread.

"You're the most handsome man I've ever seen in mine," she replies, and I can tell she's telling me the truth. I reach up and rest my fingers on her belly, splaying my hand over the spot where my child's going to be spending the next few months. Couldn't think of a better place to be. Amy stops moving, sliding her hand back out of her panties and leaning into me, eyes drooping closed with emotion. "Are you scared?" she asks, but I'm already smiling, moving my fingers to the back of her neck and pulling her down for a kiss.

"The only thing in this world I'm scared of, Amy Cross, is losing you. Everything else is a Goddamn cake walk." My tongue slides into her mouth, tasting her, absorbing her heat. We stay locked together like that, hips grinding, bodies soaked in sweat, until we find our orgasm. *Our* orgasm. Amy and I come together, like the fairytale couple that Gaine's always believed in, but I never have. Until now. Until this moment. This single, perfect Goddamn moment.

CHAPTER 35

Austin

I wake up the following morning with a big ass fucking grin on my face. I've always been a sort of vanilla motherfucker when it came to sex, but being with Amy makes me want to lay on the kink. Woo. I swear to myself that I won't ever be complaining about those romance novels of hers. No sane man would after seeing the things I seen. *Son of a motherloving bitch.*

I sit up in bed, glancing down at Amy's sleeping face. She's angelic when she's like that, all sweet and innocent. The dirty girl part's all buried beneath the surface. I bend down to kiss her forehead, trying my best to ignore the raging hard-on I got under the sheets. When the phone rings, I almost toss the damn thing out the window. Except I know better than that. We're in limbo right now, resting between disaster and success. I gotta bring this club out on top or I ain't worth my shit in salt.

"'Ello," I answer, not recognizing the number on the caller ID. Probably should've given me an indication that something was up, but I'm still sleep and sex addled. Got Amy Cross on the brain right now.

"Austin, listen to me very carefully." It's Tax. My hard-on disappears like it ain't ever been, and I swing my legs to the floor, muscles tight, anxiety wracking my brain with worry. I get this little itch in the back of my skull. *This is it. This has to be it.* With their clubhouse empty, I knew it was going to come down to this. "Broken Dallas and Bested by Crows are flying under new colors, as The Branded Kestrels MC, and they're on their way to pay you a little visit. I got a friend of a friend who runs guns on the side, and he told me he refused to sell them any shit after our little showdown. Word is though that they got another source. They still owe me for that crap they pulled at the warehouses." Tax pauses, and in the heavy silence, I can tell it's more than just that. He's worried about his little sister. "We're on our way to pay them a little visit, but it sounds like they're going to get to you first. I suggest you come up with a plan."

My heart is pounding, but I ignore it. I'm ready for

this. After months of this ridiculous fucking crap, I'm going to end it. What kind of President would I be if I didn't? I don't need to bring my baby into this shit. Time to calm the tempest.

"I got a plan, brother," I tell him, hoping he doesn't take offense at the term. This is going to be tough, ain't got no doubts about that, but it has to be done. "I've had one brewin' in my head for a while now. We'll be alright, but if you are inclined to take your vengeance today, I would much appreciate the assistance." Tax grunts and I hear the sound of bikes revving in the background. I guess when he says he's on his way, he really fuckin' means it. "But we can hold our own while we wait. Don't worry about your sister, Tax. Beck would die before he'd let anything happen to her." Tax growls.

"Yeah, well, he better considering she's eighteen fucking years old and pregnant. That's the least that son o' bitch could do for her." Tax pauses. "But we won't worry about that right now. I'll give your Sergeant at arms an earful later. Let's just try and see if you can live through the night." Tax hangs up the phone, leaving me with the gentle sound of Amy's breath and the whir of the fan.

I put my elbows on my knees, close my eyes and take a deep breath.

"Austin?" I look back at Amy and find her with a gun clutched in her small, pale hand. My pregnant woman is lying there nude with a Goddamn revolver. "Are you alright?"

"Where in the hell did that come from?" I ask, turning to face her and noticing that my erection is back. Not at all appropriate, but what the hell? Who gives a flyin' fuck? Amy smiles softly at me and shrugs gently.

"Kimmi gave it to me after I caught her and Christy kissing. I think it was supposed to keep me quiet." She smiles wickedly and lays the gun against the blankets. "But today I think it might just help to save my life." I nod at her, proud to be the man she chose to have in her life. I lean down and press my hot mouth against hers, tasting courage and love and fear. But that's what makes her brave. If you don't fear something, then rising up against it doesn't make you brave. Courageous, maybe. Strong. But not brave. To be brave, you have to fight against something that scares you. That's the rule.

"It'll be alright, Amy. I won't let anything happen to you." She smiles at me and presses her palm against the side of my face.

"I know." She sits up straight and presses a smoldering kiss to my lips again. My heart is ready for this battle, ready for it to be over, but my dick wishes we had an extra half an hour or so. I give Amy's tit a squeeze for good measure, toss her a wink and stand up. A certain cool calmness drifts over me like fog.

President.

I'm going to earn that term today, even if it kills me.

CHAPTER 36
AMY

Austin doesn't suggest that I run and hide, disappear while this battle wages at the place I'm just starting to realize truly feels like home. And I don't mean the house. The house is nice and my room is perfection, like a page torn from a magazine. What I mean, though, is Austin. Austin feels like home, and as long as my presence doesn't distract him from what he's doing, I'm going to stay by his side.

"Beck." Austin bursts into the room, using the ring of keys that leads to every room in the house. He's the only one that has a copy. I smile apologetically at Tease as she tugs the sheets over her breasts and turns to look at us over her shoulder. She's sitting in about the same position I was last night, so I understand how disturbing this must be. I pretend I don't even notice that she's straddling Beck's body, or at least that I don't know that he's probably inside of her at this moment. I keep my face stoic. "We got problems."

Right away, Tease rolls off and Beck rises to his feet. I look away from his exposed erection and again use those wonderful skills of pretending to imagine that I don't see it.

"Where?" Beck asks, voice all militaristic and harsh. When I sneak a peek at his face though, he's grinning. Austin's mouth is set in a grim but determined line. He's wearing Triple M's jacket, the black leather a nice contrast to the white T-shirt underneath. The three M's of the logo smile back at me as I touch my fingers to my own leather sleeve. I wore jeans and black boots, without heels – unfortunately, I'm no Kimmi. Austin and I essentially have dressed in matching outfits. It seems appropriate, like a military uniform or something.

"Here," Austin says as Beck spews some colorful curses and grabs a pair of jeans from the floor. He slides them on while we stand there and wait. "Broken Dallas and Bested by Crows – *The Branded Kestrels* – " Austin slurs his words, dragging his Southern drawl through the mud in disgust, "are on their way here. Now. With guns. Probably some big ones like the

M16s I saw before. Get ready. Start boarding up the inside windows, all along the back and front. Leave only enough space for a barrel or a knife to peek through. We're making a stand." Beck whoops, raising a T-shirt high, like a flag. Austin glances over at Tease. Her face is drawn and determined and I know that, like me, she won't be leaving. We fight here today, as equal members of this club, as partners to our men, as women who are allowed to be sisters in a brotherhood.

"We'll be ready in two minutes," she assures us both, nodding her chin and letting the sheets fall, as equally unembarrassed about her nakedness as her lover is. She tucks some red hair behind her ear as we turn to leave. "Or less."

Austin salutes them with a grin of his own and takes us down the hall, stopping in each room, giving orders to every single Triple M'er he passes by. Everyone is important here, and today, everyone is a part of Austin's plan. I couldn't be more proud. He's had this in him all along, has simply refused to see it. Today, he lets it shine bright.

We go downstairs next, finding Gaine and Mireya in the kitchen, beers already clutched in their hands. It might be early morning, but the rules of drink don't apply here. If anyone in this club wants a Goddamn beer, they get one. I smile.

"Get your weapons and your shit together," Austin says, pausing only briefly in front of them. "We got trouble. Our old friends are coming to settle the score, and we're going to make sure it ends in our favor. Help Beck and Tease board up the windows." Austin only pauses to take a small breath. "Where's Kimmi?" he asks as his friends set down their beers and grab some sheets of plywood that are leaning against the walls. There's no wasting time here. Everything has to be done just so, laid out just right. The goal here isn't just to *win*, I know that. Austin's told me before that his Code of the Road demands respect and requires intention. Today, we intend to show that we won't be disrespected, that this is where we stand, and that it's time to leave us the *fuck* alone. But I know that Austin isn't willing to gamble any of our forty members for that. We need to make it through this with as few lives lost and as few wounded as possible.

"At the other house," Gaine says, but we're already halfway out the door. Austin orders everyone inside, has them lock up the garage and post sentries inside to guard the bikes. We continue across the yard and straight up into the other house.

"Kimmi, we need everyone out of here and ready to stir up shit." I smile at Christy who's sitting on the end of an old countertop, blushing at me. I smile back, just to let her know that I don't care how much time she spends with Kimmi Reynolds, that even if she fell in love with her, it wouldn't matter. Heck, I smile bigger to let her know that if she *doesn't* like Kimmi, if she changes her mind, if she chooses another life, whatever, that I'll still love her. We lock gazes for a moment.

"Oh, Lord," Kimmi groans, grabbing her bag of tools and hoisting it onto her shoulder. "It's time, isn't it?" Austin nods once, briskly.

"Time to sweep Kent and his garbage and all our excess baggage under the rug and be done with it. Time to show them what we're really fucking made of."

CHAPTER 37
Austin

The worst part of any war is the waiting, the silence that precedes that single burst of sound, that explosion of action and pain and death. All of that happens in an instant so quick, it may as well be the blink of an eye. What makes it so hard, so much more painful, is all of this quiet beforehand. I've got my group positioned exactly as I want them, each person in their place, each pair of hands a cog in this ticking time machine. Amy is by my side, as she should be, as I always hope she will be. In my hands, I've got a gun.

While I sit and wait, slumped in the dark, in the back of the house, I think about how we're going to deal with the aftermath of this crap. There will be blood – lots of it – and bodies most likely. In the past, all we've had to do was run and keep running. That's the good part of being nomadic. Right now, our choices are much more limited. We're going to have to clean this up and quick, before anyone gets it in their heads to come check this out. In some places, the cops have it in for any motorcycle club that crosses their path. They will *look* for ways to bust them. Here, it's the opposite. They tend to look the other way. That's a good thing, but it doesn't last forever. Just because they can't interfere in a major firefight doesn't mean they won't come later. My only real hope here is that we're far enough away from the neighbors that we can wrap this up fast. Tease tells me Tax has a thing with cops, that he knows some folks higher up and can guarantee they'll leave us be, but I can't count on that. Besides, there's always a price for that kind of thing, and I don't know what Tax's might be.

Guess we'll figure things out when we get to 'em.

The sound of hogs roars in the distance, echoing loudly in the dead silence of our clubhouse. Nobody moves, but I feel tension rippling the air, turning the already hot room *scalding*. My fellow Triple M'ers have been waiting some time to take their anger out, and now's their chance.

I take a deep breath.

Amy puts her hand on my wrist and we exchange a

long look, one that's filled with love and understanding, one that promises that even were we to die here today, that we could never really be separated. It's exactly what I need. I raise my hand and gesture with loose fingers, pulling a select few of my guys along with me: Beck, Joel, Bryan, Kimmi, and three others. Everyone else waits in this room, one up from mine and Amy's. It's filled with furniture that lines the walls, makes this our best hope at a safe haven if it comes to heavy fire while our enemies are in the house.

Amy makes a small sound as I go, but we both know the plan, that I'll be right back here after the first wave of assaults. We've got this.

I don't ask if everyone knows the signal – they do. When I shoot, they shoot. That's it. Easy as pie. I swallow any last vestiges of fear and burn them away. There's no time for that.

Branded Kestrels pulls up on their bikes, not bothering to hide their approach. When I glance out the windows, I see why. I count maybe eighty men before my stomach dips. And there's probably a good two dozen or so more where I can't see 'em. At least, if these fuckers are smart there should be. We're going to need Seventy-seven Brothers' help, but only if we live long enough for them to get here.

"Austin Sparks." It's the man from before, with the

dark hair and eyes, the one with the goatee and the bad motherfucking case of hubris. I guess he's their new Pres, maybe their Sergeant at arms. Whatever. I don't give two flyin' fucks. He's the first one I'm going to aim for. I raise my gun to the small hole in the plywood. I know it won't give us much protection should these sons of bitches start using the M16s they're pulling out and leveling on us, but at least it makes our position almost impossible to determine from the outside. "Last chance to surrender. If you do, we'll take what we want, you'll leave and never come back. It's that or you die here today." The man pauses and a ripple of anger pauses through his still form. "You burned down a very important relic the other day and now we've got some folks that would like to see you make an even trade. Give up the clubhouse and come out, no weapons, no smart ass attitudes."

I take aim. I figured that there'd be at least a moment or two of jaw flapping before the violence got started. I'm going to cut that down to thirty seconds. I look down the row, at the other seven folks standing with me, seven folks who are all too aware that we could very well die within the next few seconds.

I put my finger on the trigger, close my eyes and breathe.

When they snap back open, my gun goes off and so

do the others alongside me. My shot goes a little wide, missing the President but hitting another man square in the chest. He drops to the pavement, taking his gun along with him. I see a few of the other bullets find their marks, and then we all take another shot. We only have time for two before the Branded Kestrels realize we're on the second floor and decide to pepper it with holes.

I don't bother to duck, but rather dive, rolling behind the row of furniture we put here just for this purpose. It won't stop all the bullets, but at least we've got something between them and us. I don't check to see if anyone's been hurt – I can't do that until after this is all over or I might not make it through. Instead I focus on crawling back towards the hallway, into the room closest to the stairs and taking aim through yet another set of holes drilled in the wall here. Our poor house is going to need a whole fuck ton of repairs after this crap is over.

CHAPTER 38
AMY

I hear the shots and bite my lip until it bleeds, praying to the gods of motorcycles that Austin will make it out of this okay. I squeeze my hand over Christy's, looking back at her with a gun in her small hand and her body shaking with fear. We had about ten minutes to figure out how to use these guns, taking a crash course with Kimmi in the backyard. I don't know how good of an aim I'll be, but at least I have it for close combat. As long as I can protect my person and keep the majority of Branded Kestrels out of this room, I'll be of assistance to the group.

Mireya keeps her gaze out the window, on the grass below, searching for anyone that might try to sneak in from the back. Her shoulders are tense, but her eyes never stray from that single purpose, not even when we hear the doors being kicked in and shouts echoing through the house.

"You fucking cowards!" I hear the screech, but I ignore it, focused solely on the doorway into this room. I have to be careful not to engage in any friendly fire, but also to stop any enemies. There are seven of us in here. That's not a lot, but we've got a small group and a big plan. I hear the swearing and cursing, slamming doors, a few stray shots, but there's nobody down there, at least not inside anyway. We have a few scattered folks hiding out back, but that's it.

It takes a moment, one that seems to stretch into forever, before we finally hear boots on the stairs. Another wave of gunfire follows that sound and there are thuds, bodies probably, crashing sounds that echo down the stairs. More shots come and then fade again as the Branded Kestrels try to figure out what's going on. Austin Sparks has done well. I liken our battle to the American Revolutionary War. On a much smaller scale, of course, but there are similarities.

"Amy, I'm scared," Christy whispers, but I can't offer her any comfort. All I can do is stay focused on this. The footsteps continue up the stairs and then there's the sound of doors being kicked in as the men search for us. They're going to find mostly empty rooms, unfortunately for them. A few moments later, another round of gunfire. The third wave shoots through the holes we drilled in the wall, firing on the men in the hallway. Different sounds follow that as the Branded Kestrels figure out where some of the Triple M'ers are hiding. Grunts and the crack of weapons replaces the sound of guns.

My breathing slows and becomes heavier as I hear Austin give a shout from the other room, drawing his friends with him, and exploding from their room in a boom of sound. I cringe, waiting for the sound of machine guns, but the quarters are too tight in here, too easy to hit one of your own and too difficult to find a target. More footsteps hit the stairs and a minute later, I see my first unfriendly face. A shot hits the man squarely in the head – definitely not mine. My first bullet goes wild, burying itself into the wall as more bodies crowd the door, flowing inward, pushing their comrades forward in a rush to overwhelm us. I start shooting then, emptying my revolver into the crowd. I hit some of the men, I think, but the feeling isn't a good one. I don't want to be doing this. I'd rather not. But I'll do whatever it takes to earn this life and my freedom, whether it's right or wrong.

I remind myself of what these men wanted to do to me, what they did to Mireya, the drug trafficking, the forced prostitution, the fight at the warehouses. I absorb everything Austin's told me about them and use it like a cloak to shield myself. I may never be the same after this, but growth is bought with change and not all change is painless. The entrance into the room and the maze of furniture we've built slow our attackers enough that the tide doesn't turn, instead evolving into a standstill, with them on one side of our makeshift walls and us on the other. Nobody moves.

I hear the scraping of boots, the reloading of guns, some cursing, some whispers. Down the hall another battle rages, but I block it out, trying to narrow my focus on this. I'm starting to crawl towards Mireya, who's since moved from the window, when a shaft of sunlight breaks across my skin, slicing sharply through the shadows. I glance over my shoulder and find a group of men climbing into the window, swelling through the opening like monsters. With them is the only woman that I've seen on their side thus far – Margot Tempe.

She sees me and raises her gun, faster than I can, and I just know then that I'm going to get shot. Time slows down and a second later, her blood is spraying the wall behind her, her body dropping like a puppet with no one to hold the strings. I glance over at Christy, breathing hard, hands quavering on the gun. *She saved my life.* She looks over at me for just a moment, before we're being assaulted from both sides. Some of the men coming in the window slump over the edge, shot by our members in the backyard, but there are still a lot of them, too many it seems.

I struggle to reload my gun, but I'm sloppy and ammo goes rolling across the floor. A man lunges at me, apparently also without his gun in proper use, and we collide. My body slams into the wall with a grunt and a knife slices up and through my arm, cutting deep but not maiming. I scream and fumble at my belt, sliding free my own knife, one that Austin gave me just this morning. If this man had wanted to kill me, he probably could have. Instead, he grabs me by my hair and drags me forward. I don't know what his intentions are – to knock me out? Take me hostage? Rape me? – but it doesn't matter. If I hesitate, I could lose everything, destroy Austin, and ruin my baby's chance at a good life, all in one fell swoop.

I stab my knife into his gut and twist. The feeling of the blade slicing through flesh is disgusting at best, disturbing at worst, but at least he lets go of my hair and stumbles backwards. I look up and find myself face to face with the barrel of a gun.

CHAPTER 39
Austin

I was right: close quarters means less gunfire and more hand to hand action. I know my Triple M'ers can swing a hammer like nobody's business, so I fight with a grin on my lips. It's not a grin of happiness, but more like a feral growl. I feel like a wolf fighting to defend his pack. I use a wrench and take up the rear, skirting around the outer edges of the scuffle and stepping up to swing my weapon at the backs of enemy skulls. The less dead folk here, the better. And I don't intend to kill *everyone*, just most of them. My real goal is to find the President. I bet after that first shot, he stayed back from the melee. Now I just have to find him.

When I decide that we're on the winning end in here, I move away, skirting down the hallway and coming to the door of Amy's room just in time to see a gun pointed at her face. My own gun comes up and out of its holster, and I fire a shot. The man collapses onto the floor, bleeding from the neck. Amy looks up at me and even with all the bullshit swirling around us, we lock eyes.

I move into the room and help Mireya and the others take out the last few stragglers.

"I've gotta find their Pres," I say without preamble. No time for that shit. "Let's go." The Triple M'ers that are left in that room follow me without complaint. I don't get time to count them all, but I hear more than just my friends' footsteps behind me as we descend down the stairs. I glance back, just once, to see Amy, Mireya, and Christy on my heels. When I hit the first floor, Gaine is waiting for me.

"There's a small group outside." Gaine purses his lips. "With their M16s at the ready, of fuckin' course." I move past him and peek around the window. The plywood in the front is still in place, so I gesture for everyone else to wait while I scoot forward and take a look out the narrow slat. The President of Branded Kestrels is still standing there, but he looks nervous. As I watch, he climbs on his bike and gestures for the remaining members of his club to follow. There're about a dozen of them, but that's alright. I wait for them to put their guns away and start their engines. As soon as they turn to head down the street, I pull the group forward with a wave of my hand, step out onto the porch and take a shot.

The Pres' back tire explodes and his bike swerves, crashing to the ground in the spin of wheels and the sound of screeching metal. A few of the other guys go down, rolling off their bikes and landing in painful crashes on the ground not two houses down from us. To the detriment of their honor and credit, the last few remaining members don't stop but keep riding, disappearing into the distance. I figure we don't have to worry about them anymore.

"My fucking leg!" The man is screaming, writing in agony under this trapped bike. Without waiting for the others, I move over to him, listening as the sounds inside the house go still, and more Triple M'ers begin emerging from the shadows. As I stand over the man with the dark hair, the one who made a fatal Goddamn mistake by coming here, I hear the sound of motorcycles. *Seventy-seven Brothers.*

I gesture at Gaine and he helps me pull the man out from under his ride, disarm him and stand him up to face the growing crowd at gunpoint. I wait until most everyone is out here, Amy by my side, my friends reunited with their lovers, and Tax standing proud by his sister, his men a vast sea of color in the background.

"Triple M has never been a particularly large MC, or an influential one, but we're held together by the hearts and the determination of our members." I look down at Amy, at her soft hair billowing in the breeze and her beautiful half-smile. "We won't be bullied, disrespected, or fucked with. We won't be kept down or pushed out of sight, and we won't give up." I reach down and squeeze Amy's hand, hating what I have to do but knowing I'm going to do it anyway.

I look at the President from Branded Kestrels, the motorcycle club that only lasted a minute, and I don't care that I don't know his name or where he's from. All I know is that this is my ultimate act as President, my chance to show my strength, and be the leader my friends want me to be.

"You sir, have committed so many wrongs here today. You've dishonored yourself and your brotherhood with your cowardly actions and your failed chance at escape." I hold my gun to his head and watch as urine soaks the front of his pants. My finger pulls the trigger but nothing happens. It's not an accident that my gun holds no ammo. This here was done on purpose. "But I won't shed another drop of blood today, not one extra driblet of red in this squabble. Now get your ass out of my territory and go. If I ever see you again, I *will* change my mind." I put my gun away, nod at Gaine, and we both watch as the man stumbles in his terror, limping through the neighborhood with nothing and no one at his side.

I look down at Amy and find her eyes filled with tears. My hands come to rest on either side of her face, and the breath between us heats with fire just an instant before our mouths touch. In the background, I hear nothing but the sound of cheers.

Epilogue

Happily ever after.

It's a phrase you often find in the end of books, but not in real life. Happily ever after is a hard thing to determine because every day is new, bringing with it fresh challenges and hard-earned triumphs. But sometimes, you just know that no matter what happens, you won't regret the moment you're in right now, the perfection of the present, the enjoyment of a single second that feels like it should stretch on forever. That's how I determine that I'm going to have my happily ever after.

I look down at the ring on my finger and then up at the backyard. It's more like a park really, a winding pathway dotted with bushes, trees, the bodies of old motorcycles laid to rest. Flowers grow in circles around them, like they're statues, presented in this mess of green as decorations, testaments to who we are and where we come from.

"Look at you, my lovely little pregnant wife." Austin Sparks appears next to me, drenched in sweat, covered in spots of oil. He leans down, his leather jacket creaking as he kisses me full on the lips, searing me with heat and cutting through straight to my heart, blinding me with the lingering taste of love that rests on his lips. "Enjoying the weather?"

"Trying to get in another few rays of sunshine before this baby comes." I touch my fingers to my swollen belly while the sound of laughter rings in my ears. Children come winding up the path, flying across the gravel with their shoes crunching on the rocks. Four of them in total, not all mine, of course. Only one of those is mine, the little girl with the sandy blonde hair and the bright blue eyes. Then there's Beck and Tease's redheaded little twins, and Gaine and Mireya's surprise. "Is Christy feigning a headache again?" I ask as Austin slides into the seat next to me and holds his hand out for mine. We got married back here, you know, so this is a special spot for us.

I set my eReader aside, pausing at a very dirty passage in my book, so that I can enjoy the moment. It took Austin nearly a year after we moved into the clubhouse to propose to me, but he did it right, on the back of a motorcycle in the club's colors, with a grin on his crooked mouth. I squeeze his hand and smile.

"She is," he replies, leaning his head against the back of the chair and closing his eyes. "She says she doesn't want to watch this birth anymore than she wanted to see the last. My guess is that she's going to have a continuous headache until *after* the baby's born. If she's too sick to go, well, you know." He chuckles.

"Did Tax and Melissa stop by?" I ask, changing the subject. If Christy doesn't want to go, that's alright. Kimmi will come to the hospital whether Christy wants to or not, and she'll follow. They're inseparable that way. Besides, I'll have no shortage of people by my side, most importantly my husband, Austin Sparks. And my mama, of course. She'll be there, too. If all of Triple M could come, they probably would. Well, most of them anyway. I grin at the thought of Beck passing out cold on the floor of Tease's delivery room. Everyone has their weaknesses.

"They did. Melissa returned some book that you lent her, and she hinted that Seventy-seven Brothers might be pushing to expand their territory. There's a club between us and them that's been trafficking in some dark ass shit. *Should the Need Arise*, I guess. I told 'em I didn't mind." Austin opens his eyes and lifts his head, smiling at our daughter as she thunders past, raising my fingers to his mouth for one, perfect, little kiss. "Anything that makes the world safer for y'all makes me a happy, happy man." I give him a look that he pretends he doesn't see.

"No motorcycle rides until she's ten," I say sternly. "If you care that much about safety, you'll listen to me on this one."

"Four," he counters. I raise an eyebrow. "Five?"

"You really are insufferable, you know that?" I ask and Austin grins big.

"Sugar, if you're willing to put up with me, that's all that really matters. You say ten, then I'll wait until she's fifteen."

"I love you, Austin Sparks," I say.

"And I love you, too, Amy Cross."

Never were truer words spoken.

And so we lived happily ever after.

The End

Dear Reader,

Thank you for joining me and following along with Triple M's growth from nomadic bikers to one big, happy family. I had considered more books in the series – with Kimmi and Christy or Tax and Melissa – but it felt right to end it here. With a happily ever after. And also with the characters who started it all, back when *Losing Me, Finding You* changed from a stand-alone novel to a four book series.

I hope you enjoyed the ride, the love, the sex, the shootouts. And I also hope you'll join me on my next adventure. These characters might have found their happiness, but there are a whole host of others stuck in my head desperate to get out. Follow me on Facebook @ www.facebook.com/cmstunichauthor for all the latest news, or email me here: author@cmstunich.com if you have any questions about these books or any others.

And last but not least, I heart the hell out of you.

Thanks for reading.

Love, C.M. Stunich

P.S. Even though this is the final book in this series, there's so much more I'd like to share with you. If you have time or space in your inbox, I'm going to be starting a once a month newsletter with new release info, sales, and giveaways. The sign up form can be found here:

https://www.facebook.com/cmstunichauthor/app_100 265896690345

Hell Inc.

...Dating is hell. Then again, so are yetis, fairies and socio-paths...

AMAZON BESTSELLING AUTHOR
C.M. STUNICH

Excerpt Included!

Chapter 1

It's never easy to deal with supernatural creatures, especially when they've got the IQ of a doormat. And the clerk behind the counter wasn't your typical teenage drop out. Nope. This one was a special one. He glared at me with his one eye (which just happened to be lazy and seemed to be staring at the ridiculously bright fluorescent lights above my head instead of at my drowsy face) while I questioned him as to the whereabouts of a very specific item. I was looking for black candles. Spooky, huh? But that's what the newspaper ad had specified and so, that's what I was going to get.

"Um," the clerk, who I suspected was probably a Cyclops, mumbled under his garlic scented breath. It was so bad that I actually had to take a step away from him, press my spine against a display of cheap romance novels, and choke back a sob. His breath was so terrible, in fact, that I thought I saw a puff of green float out past his thin lips and join the CFC gasses in destroying the ozone layer. "I think we've got some Glade Flameless Candles in the clearance aisle. They're eggplant purple, but they look black." I tried not to scowl. The Cyclops didn't know what I needed them for. I thanked him politely and wandered off. Served me right for trying to go to Target for dark arts supplies.

I found the aisle my halitosis challenged friend had been talking about and stared at the little white boxes with their red clearance stickers. *Yeah*, I thought sourly, feeling defeated before I'd even begun. *That's what the Devil wants, candles without flames. In eggplant. Fantastic.* I scooped several of the boxes into my basket anyway and tried to ignore the pixies that were swooping and giggling and pulling my mussy hair. If I swatted at them, if I paid them the tiniest bit of attention, then they would do worse. Had done worse. Focus, attention, *belief*, it was what made them real.

When a girl and her mother sauntered into the aisle, tossing their identical peroxide manes and glaring at my ripped jeans and my faded *Shrek* T-shirt, they walked right through them.

The pixies giggled and darted towards their shopping basket, shedding sticky glitter dust all over the white linoleum as they heaved a packet of pens out, twiggy arms straining with the effort, and dropped them on the floor. The mother picked them up absently, hardly noticing what she was doing. I sighed. How nice it would be to live so ignorantly. To not know that anything other than humans walked this world. I squinted my gaze at the shelf and tried not to kick something. It wasn't fair. It just wasn't fair.

But this was why I was doing this. Following the directions in this stupid ad. I picked at my pants pocket until I found the crumbled square of newsprint. As I reread it, I couldn't help but have terrible flashbacks to Brendan Fraser and *Bedazzled*. But he'd been stupid. He hadn't been clear with his wishes. I would be. I'd rattle 'em off like the best of bureaucrats. The key was to be *specific*. Very, very specific. I mouthed the words aloud as I walked, swinging my basket and trying to stay positive.

"WANTED: Souls. Single adults only. We are a professional organization looking for talented persons of marriageable age to enter into a trade agreement. Willing to offer three wishes in exchange for a signed contract. Please contact us at our office by arranging three black candles into a semi-circle in front of a mirror. Anoint with blood. Recite address. Hell Incorporated, 666 Gladiola Lane. This solicitation posted by the Devil. No sales inquiries. Offer ends 08/16."

Okay, so it sounded shady and well, just plain bizarre, but I was getting desperate. Two years out of high school had left me with a crappy apartment and a crappier job. I had no friends (except for Erin, but I didn't even really like her), my family was too busy to ever come and see me (and I never went to see them either, I know, I know), and I had absolutely no romantic prospects of which to speak. Well, there was this guy that worked at our local museum, William T. Smidden's Palace of History, that was pretty smoking hot, but I knew I didn't stand a chance. He always had this group of people swarming around like he was the queen bee, buzzing and nodding and kissing his ass. He was young with sandy hair and a strong jaw and pale eyes that shimmered like the aquamarine jewel on my pinky finger. I raised my hand to my lips and gave the ring a light kiss, pretending for just a moment that it was that man's mouth, confident and strong.

I was so entranced in my thoughts that I forgot about the pixie dust and ended up slipping, rather comically, my legs flying out from under me, worn rubber soles of my shoes parallel with the ceiling for just a moment before I ended up slamming into the floor so hard that I was seeing stars. I knew it was bad because the stars weren't just spots of light; they were yellow and smiling and singing the theme song to *My Little Pony*.

The Cyclops I had spoken with earlier raced towards me, red vest flapping, as he pounded over to me and knelt quickly, waving a hand in front of my face and asking a bunch of stupid questions that I wouldn't have known the answer to even if I hadn't just given myself a concussion.

I waved him away but ended up with the store manager and several rubber necking customers surrounding me, jabbering away, and making my head spin while the pixies laughed and sprinkled more of their sparkling crap over my face and arms. I'd be visible from space for the next week. I groaned and sat up while the manager sweated and mumbled things about lawsuits. I rubbed my head and pointed at my basket, just wanting to get the heck out of there.

"I won't sue you," I said, pointing at the candles and trying not to drool. "But can I have these for free?" The manager licked his lips and nodded. *This is too easy,* my brain tried to convince me. *Ask for more.* "And do you happen to have any chicken blood?"

* * *

A half an hour later, I was strolling out the automatic doors of the Super Target and mouthing the lyrics to some pop song that I only actually knew half the words to. They hadn't had any chicken blood, but they had given me several containers of chicken hearts. There seemed to be quite a bit of bloody residue sloshing about in the bottom of the Styrofoam containers, so I decided that would count. It would have to. It was getting late, and today was the sixteenth, the last day for me to try the spell.

I trudged up the rickety, cement steps to my apartment and tried to ignore the permanent smell of moth balls and dog urine that seemed to permeate the dreary hallway. My neighbor, Gene, a lady of questionable age with a sneer as sharp as cheddar and a smell to match, kicked open her door and proceeded to glare at me as I fumbled around with my keys. She always did that. Opened her door and stared at me. I think on some deep level that she recognized that there was something different about me. Sometimes people did. Though they never seemed to be able to get what that was. If only I felt confident enough in my own sanity to share the simple fact that I could see things that they didn't. I sighed and managed to get into the eight hundred square foot shit hole before Gene began shouting. She did that, too, sometimes. But that was only because she was crazy. She shouted at everyone: the super, the PG&E guy, the mail lady. That act wasn't just reserved for me.

I slammed the door behind me, locked it, handle, dead bolt, chain, always in that order, and headed immediately for my bedroom. If I was going to meet the Devil, I was going to do it in style.

I found a slinky, skin tight dress as red as a hooker's lipstick, and since I'd bought it used at Goodwill, probably something that had actually been worn by a hooker, and paired that with some black pumps and a quick slash of eyeliner. I grinned at myself in the wavy mirror that hung crookedly on the back of my bedroom door. I was as hot as a book cover bimbo. Perfect. I fluffed my black bob, punctuated by neon streaks of pumpkin-bright orange, courtesy of Punky Colour, and sashayed into the bathroom. I was in a better mood than the day I'd bought my Rabbit Habit, though not by much.

The candles, once I'd taken them out of eight, stiff, plastic layers of protection and about a dozen twist ties, looked absolutely ridiculous arranged around the edge of the porcelain sink in my bathroom. They flickered weakly, the cheap lights inside dimming and brightening in a pathetic imitation of a true candle. I frowned at them as I opened the plastic top to the chicken hearts. They smelled gamey and a little bit like iron, leaving a heavy, metallic burn in the back of my throat.

"God," I choked as I dipped two fingers into the cold, watery bird blood. My spine bucked involuntarily as I rubbed the runny ooze down the side of one candle, and then the next, and the next. Let's just say it didn't get any easier or any less disgusting.

After I was finished, I tossed the unused hearts into the bathroom garbage can and scraped anything resembling so much as a fingerprint off of my skin in an attempt at cleansing myself. Once I had decided that liquid soap, a squirt of shampoo, and half a travel sized bottle of Purell would just about do it, I was ready to begin.

I flicked the lights off and grabbed the newspaper scrap off its temporary home on the back of the toilet. I squinted at the words which were incredibly difficult to read in the flickering light and took a deep breath.

"Hell Incorporated," I began, trying to pitch my voice low so that it came out as eery and mysterious as possible. "666 Gladiola Lane." I set the newspaper down on the edge of the sink next to one of the plastic eggplant monstrosities and waited. And waited. And waited.

Nothing happened.

"Goddamn it," I screeched at myself, fighting back tears and gripping the sides of the mirror with a frenzied fervor. "Why do I do this to myself?"

I had a tendency to get really, *really* involved in things that most people could tell weren't going to work out for the best. It was one of my special talents. I punched the mirror once, in a juvenile fight of rage, cracking the glass and cutting my hand open along with it. Tiny droplets of red dripped into the sink and swirled down the drain, turning the residual water a pinkish color and staining the edges of the white porcelain.

"Ah, hell," I cursed, unaware of the swirling black vortex beneath my feet. "I'm going to need stitches."

And then I was falling down a hole, screaming like a B-list actress in a horror movie, until I found myself landing face first onto some terribly itchy, navy carpeting. I pushed myself up quickly, tugging down my dress in the back in an attempt to cover my ass, before taking a look around.

My exploration ended before it even got started because the very first thing I saw was the demon.

C.M. Stunich

And he was pissed.

About the Author

C.M. Stunich was raised under a cover of fog in the area known simply as Eureka, CA. A mysterious place, this strange, arboreal land nursed Caitlin's (yes, that's her name!) desire to write strange fiction novels about wicked monsters, magical trains, and Nemean Lions (Google it!). She currently enjoys drag queens, having too many cats, and tribal bellydance.

She can be reached at author@cmstunich.com, and loves to hear from her readers. Ms. Stunich also wrote this biography and has no idea why she decided to refer to herself in the third person.

Happy reading and carpe diem!

www.cmstunich.com

12441243R00180

Made in the USA
San Bernardino, CA
16 June 2014